Closure

Closure

Sylvia Stein

Contents

Closure

By Sylvia Stein

Chapter One

Oct 15, 1999

Dear Diary,

I will never forget the day my mother passed away. I can recall that moment as if it were yesterday.

My life changed forever.

There was once a time when I thought life was perfect. After all, my mother and father were high school sweethearts. It seemed like they would be together forever.

Or so I thought.

Sadly, for our family, it was not to be.

Her death was the beginning of a nightmare . . . my nightmare.

Like most children, I did not understand the concept of time. There were many nights when the side effects of my mother's chemo woke our family. I could hear her coughs and knew she was in pain. She attempted to mask it from us, but there are some things you cannot hide.

Mother developed breast cancer. It runs in her side of the family, and something I must watch for. Breast cancer is not the monster of my nightmares. That monster is my father.

One day, my mother was there, and the next day—I am walking into a big home and facing a large box.

For the longest time, I stood holding my father's hand while looking at our reflection on the shiny wooden box.

The room began to fill with noise.

Confused, I looked over my shoulder and faced a dark, blue curtain.

"What's that Daddy?" I asked.

"Everyone is coming to say goodbye."

"Who's goin' away?"

He picked me up.

Inside was my mother, she looked peaceful.

Mommy is sleeping, I thought.

Delighted to see her with color and resting. I turned and whispered into my father's ear, "Ssshhhh! Mommy is sleeping. Daddy, she's not sick no more."

"Sweetie," he whispered. A jagged breath and wet heat caressed my ear.

Daddy's crying?

Lost for words, I patted his back.

His sobs deepened.

"Oh, Sara. Mommy's going away, but don't worry, we're still a family."

Young and confused, nothing made sense. My father

was crying, my mother was in a box, and people behind a curtain were there to say goodbye. Mother looked good, happy and without pain. How could someone who finally looked peaceful decide to leave?

The curtains opened.

Lost and confused, I searched the room for help.

Father carried me to the first seat and sat me down.

A strange man stood and described how wonderful my mother was. The air, the room, and, well, everything felt wrong.

Mommy is there! Why does he keep saying she is with God? I want my mom! my mind shouted.

I tried to talk but tears and the world consumed me.

Then I saw a man with a collar come up to my father and whispered something in his ear. Moments later, the man closed the lid to the box my mom was in.

Five men and my father picked up mommy's box and began carrying it out of the room. Angered by strangers carrying that infernal box, I ran in front of their path and tried to stop them.

Before I could say a word, a large, warm hand swallowed mine.

Startled, I tried to scream, but saw into my father's heartbroken eyes.

"It'll be alright," my father assured me.

He lied.

Thanks to him and his abuse, I live with night terrors, have panic attacks, and suffer from stress-induced grand mal seizures. Over time, I have lost hope, and do not know if I will ever feel normal again.

~Sara

Chapter Two

In the dark corner of a room, Sara James waited until the monster fell asleep.

Who was the monster?

Garrison James, her father.

It amazed her how much had changed in the few short months since her mother, Lila left. It felt as if it happened over night.

At first, he seemed absent. Then the yelling, drinking, and angry glares erupted whenever she entered the same room as him. Soon, he began calling her names. When she thought things could not get worse, the real abuse began.

He's not my dad! He's a monster!

Heavy footsteps tromped towards the room. She gulped in jagged breaths and looked to the ceiling while blinking rapidly. A feeble attempt to control her tears.

When hiding from the monster, she would replay what she did wrong and how he caught her the time before.

Don't cry, she reminded herself, *that's how he finds you.*

She looked around the once lively home for a sweet reminder of better times. There was a time when the house was surrounded by a beautiful garden. She and her mother would walk hand in hand and choose which flowers to bring inside. Now, the windows were closed, and the vase that usually held flowers sat empty. No matter where she looked, there was no sign of happiness or life.

The house had become a vessel of sorrow and pain.

Mommy, think of her.

She closed her eyes and forced images of her favorite memories. A brief smile appeared as thoughts reverted her to one of the many times when her mother taught her how to bake cookies.

"Oh, Momma, I miss you," she whispered.

The memory of her mother distracted Sara from the harsh reality. However, nearly as quick as the memories arrived, they dissipated, and before she knew it, the monster began lashing out.

"Sara! Sara! Where are you?" he screamed.

Realizing she had made noise. Sara covered her mouth and began internally praying.

Oh, Lord, help me!

"Where are you?" the monster demanded as he stormed towards the back of the house.

She looked up at the ceiling and whispered, "What does he want now?"

She knew he was drunk. Usually by the this time of day, he would be asleep, but his current drunken rage lasted much longer than the other nights.

"Please Lord, make him go to sleep," she begged.

"What was that," the monster bellowed.

She brought her index finger to her lips and made a shushing sound. She feared "the monster" honing in on the sound of her prayer.

A sigh escaped her when he stormed pass the room and into the kitchen.

Her stomach roared to life.

When was the last time I ate? She wondered.

For months, Sara was constantly exhausted and hungry.

When the monster moved towards the dining room, she decided to try to sneak into the kitchen. Just as she neared the threshold, she heard his footsteps and quickly reverted to her safe, hiding place.

"Sara! Come here this second," he ordered in anger.

She knew that tone all too well. If he got ahold of her, pain would soon follow.

Immediately, her heart began to race as her small body convulsed.

Her mind screamed, *NOT AGAIN!*

The last time her body shook uncontrollably, she was hiding in the closet. The monster heard her praying.

He whipped the door open and lashed out at her.

She recalled something hard striking the side of her head. It was late, and although she could not recall what hit her. She noticed a high pitch ringing sound that seemed to go on for days. When the ringing became too much, she asked her father to take her to the doctor.

He refused.

Since her mother left, her father stopped taking her to church. He said that God was a myth. She knew better. She believed in God and knew there was a doctor at the church she could see for free.

That was the only time she talked back to her father. She said he was wrong, and they should go so God can forgive him.

That was when the monster took over.

She recalled the pain she felt as he backhanded her. Moments later, her body began shaking, and then blackness set in.

When she woke, she was soaked in urine with the monster barking orders. The high pitch ringing was so loud it caused pain behind her eyes.

She learned her lesson. Instead of complaining, Sara did what the monster demanded, which was scrub the floors and make his dinner.

Her mind screamed, *Do what he says and don't fall asleep!*

Fear stricken by memories of that day, Sara's heart raced faster as her body rapidly convulsed. She needed a distraction. She again searched the room for a small piece of solace.

Closure

The house was in shambles.

Sara tried to clean, but at the age of seven, it was impossible for her to maintain the house the way her mother had.

"There you are!"

She recoiled to the corner and covered her face. Sara began cringing the closer he neared. Knowing he found her made Sara drop to her knees in fear. She gagged as the intrusive stench of alcohol and vomit crashed into her.

"Oh, Mama. If you could see what he's done to us. Oh how I wish you were still here," she cried in a whisper.

Once again, Sara's only hope was the drunken monster passing out before he hurt her. She could not get used to his verbal abuse and violent tantrums.

Since her mother left, it became her responsibility to clean up after him. Unfortunately, she could not do anything when he was awake.

Her only hopes were that the nightmare would end. Sadly, for Sara, Garrison was not about to let up. She clenched her fists as the sound of his voice echoed closer.

"Damn you! You stupid girl, I told you not to throw my bottles away!"

She could not understand how he could not remember the bottles were empty.

Garrison approached the room and stood by the doorway.

"Father, please forgive me," she begged.

"Get out of my sight now!"

"Please, Daddy!"

"Go to your room, before I make you go."

Although she did not understand what he meant, she did not question. She bolted as fast as her little legs could move.

To Sara, there were many times when he could have chosen to be there as a father.

It never happened.

She knew he loved the bottle more than family.

When she made it to the stairs without getting hit, she recalled a time when Garrison had promised to watch over her.

She glanced at him and wondered, *did he lie? No, he forgot his promise. When he drinks, he forgets everything.*

All of those memories began to take its toll on the young, malnourished girl. She was starving and needed something to eat before heading to her room.

She attempted a final plea.

"Father, please," she begged, "I am hungry."

"I told you to get out of my sight," he screamed.

She ran upstairs as fast as she could.

For a brief moment guilt crossed over Garrison.

He picked up one of the surviving family pictures and looked into the eyes of Lila. Something warm tickled his cheek. He brought his hand up and wiped away a tear.

"Get a hold of yourself. She's never coming back."

He stomped to the couch and snatched an old bottle off the table.

Closure

"Screw it," he mumbled while bringing the bottle to his lips.

Once in her room, Sara sat on her bed and fought to control her sobbing.

If he falls asleep, I can eat and clean.

"Sara, I am not going to repeat myself again!" Yelled Garrison.

He didn't say anything!

"Didn't you hear me, you pathetic girl?"

As his steps grew closer, Sara began to feel pressure on her chest and fought to gulp in a breath of air.

"What is happening to me?" she asked.

Panicked by unfamiliar pain and her inability to breathe, she whispered, "Mama, please help me."

"You don't have a mother," the monster coldly stated.

Chapter Three

It was a cold November day. Sara met with a client in her hometown.

Before leaving, she decided to pay respects to her mother's grave.

She placed flowers in front of the headstone.

As she pulled the old flowers away, she noticed there was dirt on her hand and sleeve.

"That's just great," she mumbled while taking a small bottle of hand sanitizer out of her purse.

Instantaneously, a flashback of her mother began playing in her mind. The smell of the sanitizer triggered her memory. It seemed whenever she used it, she would picture her mother lying in a hospital bed, with the overwhelming scent of antiseptic surrounding her.

She could not stand that smell, but her clients liked

it. It made them feel more confident with a caterer who constantly sanitized their hands.

For Sara, it was a double-edged sword.

As she rubbed her hands together, she drifted back to the day her mother shared the news of her illness.

She recalled hearing her father's haunting cries.

"No," he shouted repeatedly.

Sara ran into the room just in time to see him kick his chair.

"This can't be! You were supposed to get better!"

"Garrison, please. You heard the doctors. They said we could try. It didn't work."

"No! They need to run more tests."

"They did. Honey, you need to be strong. Do it for our family," Lila begged.

"They're wrong," Garrison bellowed. "We'll find another doctor. A doctor who knows what he's doing."

"We don't have much time," Lila said in her weakened state. "For months you're constantly out. I know you're hurting and I'm sorry, but I'm tired. Don't make this harder than it has to be. Stay home, Garrison, please . . . Sara needs you . . . I need you."

"I'm sorry," Garrison snapped, "I can't watch you di—I just can't do it!"

He turned and bolted out of the room.

Sara watched as her father ran past her with tears streaming down his face. He shot out of the house before she could say a word. It was something she had never witnessed before. She felt sorry for him.

"Mama?" she called out.

"Yes."

"Is Daddy alright?"

"You must not worry. He is fine."

"But he was—" Lost for words she stepped into the bedroom and asked, "Are you sure?"

"Yes," Lila replied with a comforting smile. "Daddy doesn't like it when we're sick. That's all. He wants things back to normal."

She felt a sense of guilt when she recalled her mother's smile.

Mama, you tried so hard to hide your pain. I wish I could have done more to help you. Even though I was young, I knew something was wrong, but didn't understand what it was.

She sighed heavily and admitted, "After you left, Father was never the same."

A chill washed over her as memories of the monster's rage succumbed her.

"Sara, Sara where are you?" bellowed the monster.

In her mind, she was the scared little girl she hated being. She ducked as a beer bottle shattered against the wall just inches above her head.

As fast as her legs would allow, she bolted upstairs and dove into her bedroom closet.

I hope he doesn't find me in here.

Since the day he began hitting her, she made a secret

hiding place in the very back of her closet that nobody, not even her own father could see without a flashlight.

Many nights she slept in that confined corner while waiting for him to pass out.

"Sara you come out this instance," he yelled.

Many times, he was so drunk that he would pass out before climbing the stairs. In the morning, he had no recollection of the night before.

She continued to sit in front of the cold tombstone and mourn the loss of her family.

"Damn him. He ruined everything." She looked at the stone and said with determination, "Momma, I'm here to say goodbye. I will always love and miss you, but I cannot visit or be near him anymore. He's not the same man. My father left the day after you died."

She stood and brushed the grass off her knees.

An eerie feeling of someone watching had her search the grounds.

Stop it! You're no longer that girl, she reminded herself. *He doesn't know you're here. I doubt he remembers your name.*

She turned back to the stone. Her fingertips gently caress the top as she said, "I am sorry, Momma, but this is goodbye. It is time for me to move on."

With a final nod, she grabbed her purse and headed towards her car.

Once inside, she looked into the rearview mirror and locked eyes with her reflection.

"Like the good doctor said, 'it is time for me to start living', and that's just what I'll do."

Chapter Four

The day of reckoning began like any other day. Not to say that Sara's life was normal, but with everything that she had faced, she lost the one thing nobody should go without.

Hope.

She was in survivor mode, which meant she did her best to stay out of her father's way. That is why she was surprised when she got home from school and did not see her father passed out on the couch.

Instead, she noticed the house was cleaner than when she left.

Terrified that something was wrong, she tiptoed to the stairs. She thought she would hide until she knew for sure the monster was asleep.

The third step creaked. She made a shushing sound, but it was too late, the monster heard it.

"Sara, come in here," he shouted, "I have some news."

"What is happening now?" she whispered.

She was worried.

Garrison was normally asleep when she got home from school. He expected her to have the house clean by the time he got up and began drinking again.

This day was different. Everything was different.

He doesn't sound right.

"Sara," he called again.

She hesitated before joining him.

"Father, is everything alright?"

He greeted her with a smile, and then began expressing his new outlook on life. As he continued to explain his plan, she noticed he shaved. He smelled good, and was wearing a nice suit, much like the one he wore to her mother's funeral.

"I don't believe this," she whispered.

While continuing to explain his new outlook, Garrison began walking around the house picking up empty bottles and cans.

Are we dying?

She nearly walked into him when he abruptly stopped in the center of the hallway.

He looked down at her and smiled.

Confused by actions, she carefully backed away.

"So what do you think?" he asked.

"Is—is everything alright?"

"Everything is fine my dearest girl."

For a moment, she thought he might be sincere, but

something in his eyes warned her. She did not know if he was scared for her or him. All she knew was that something was off.

"Am I dying?" she asked.

"What?"

"Will I be okay?"

"Sara, please, sit down."

"Sure," she cautiously replied. The moment she sat, she noticed a slight tremble in his hand. "Father, are you okay?"

"I'm fine," he shouted.

Here it comes. He's going to—

"I'm sorry," he said, interrupting her in mid thought.

Surprised by his apology, she blurted, "Just tell me what it is!"

"We're going to have company. Aunt Valerie is on her way."

He did not have to repeat his words.

We'll finally be free!

"I don't want Valerie to misunder—or to get..."

He stopped talking and looked straight ahead, although to Sara, it felt as if he was looking through her.

After an uncomfortable moment, she asked, "To get what?"

"To get the wrong idea!" He leaned forward and slowly muttered, "Do you understand?"

She'll understand. She's just like my mom and she cares.

"Anyway—that was all, my dear." He forced a smile.

"I hear you."

Aunt Valerie will help get rid of the monster. She felt as if a huge symphony was playing in the background. *This is great news! Momma said Aunt Valerie promised to watch over us.*

"Well, now that the cat is out of the bag. Do you have any questions?" her father asked.

We don't have a cat.

She noticed he was waiting for a reply. Her mind raced to try and find his question.

"Umm . . . no? I am fine."

I hope that's the right answer, or was I supposed to get the cat from the bag?

"Good, now go get dressed. Valerie will be here any minute."

As Sara headed upstairs, she could hardly contain her excitement.

"We are finally going to be free!"

Since her mother's passing, Sara's dreamed of the day her father returned. She thought with Valerie back, her wish would finally come true.

Don't get your hopes up, her inner voice warned. *He tricked you before, back when he was drinking in the barn.*

She paused and thought it over.

"I will not lie for the monster," she said with determination. "One day, I won't be afraid and I'll tell everyone."

Closure

Garrison called up the stairs, "Wear the purple dress Valerie sent you."

She rushed to her closet and pulled out the dress.

It had been a long time since anyone visited. She missed having friends, playing in the garden, and visits from relatives.

There was a time when kids would come over, but that was when their home was inviting. Now that very same house was the only house on the street that showed no signs of life.

She was not allowed to open the curtains. The grass was dead, and the garden held weeds nearly as tall as her father.

While changing, Sara's mind raced.

Now that Aunt Valerie is back, maybe life will be good again! She froze in place. *What if this is a visit and they haven't moved back? Should I tell her what's happening or do I pretend everything's good?*

Devastated by the loss of her sister, Valerie spiraled into a depression. She began therapy, and, soon after, her husband's work presented an opportunity to expand his career. When she called Garrison, he expressed his happiness and assured her that Sara would understand.

Valerie foolishly believed him.

It doesn't matter, Sara thought. *What matters is she's here. She'll listen. This is our chance to get help. Aunt Valerie will believe me.*

The doorbell rang.

"Sara, Sara," called her father. There was a nervous tone in his voice.

She's here!

As fast as she could, she raced to brush her hair and finish getting ready.

The dress was a little tight, but she did not care. When she stepped out of her room, she heard a familiar laugh. It was almost as if nothing had changed. That was, until she got to the top of the stairs and the familiar stench of alcohol reminded her of the truth.

"I'm coming," she shouted before skipping downstairs.

Valerie peered around the bannister.

"Sara! It's good to see you," she exclaimed.

"She is the splitting image of her mother," said Garrison.

For some reason, seeing her aunt gave Sara a sense of liberation. She pictured Valerie slaying the monster.

I'll do it, I'll tell her everything.

With her shoulders back and her head high, Sara stopped in front of Valerie and smiled brightly.

Valerie pulled her into a tight hug and chimed, "Goodness, I've missed you so much."

"I am sure you gals have a lot of catching up to do," said Garrison, "I'll check on dinner."

Without meaning to, Sara gasped when she heard him mention dinner. He had not cooked since before her mother died.

Closure

How come I didn't smell the food? Valerie noticed her puzzlement. She pulled back and scanned Sara's face.

After an uncomfortable moment, she gave a quick nod and said, "Yes—I am sure there is a lot of catching up we girls need to do."

Something in her tone worried Garrison. "Actually," he said, "I'm sure it's ready. Let's eat."

Sara clasped her aunt's hand. She feared the monster returning before she had a chance to warn her.

Garrison noticed.

He shot her a daunting glare and mumble, "Here we go."

The moment they sat down, flashbacks of dinner with her parents began rushing through Sara's mind. Soon, there was a nurse joining them, and then her mother and the nurse disappeared. She watched as wrinkles and bags formed around her father's eyes, his skin and hair drained of color, and then, the monster replaced her father.

In a matter of seconds, her entire life flashed through her mind. She noticed her hand tremble as she reached for her fork. She made a tight fist and hid it under the table.

NO! NO! NO! Her mind screamed as she searched for something to focus on.

I don't like those shakes. I don't want to bite myself or wakeup in a puddle! I have to get out of here.

Valerie noticed. She reached over and placed a hand on Sara's shoulder. "Are you alright?" she asked.

"I am sorry, Aunt Val," she cried, "I have to—"

"Oh, honey, what do you have to be sorry about? I'm the one who's sorry. I should have stayed."

From the moment Valerie placed her hand on Sara's shoulder the trembling began to calm down. It did not entirely dissipate.

"Sara's just tired. She does a lot of schoolwork," Garrison nervously stated.

Something clicked inside Sara. He fear quickly converted into strength and courage. "I'm not tired! You know the truth. Tell her! Nobody will look or listen to me. Tell her, Father. Tell her—Aunt Valerie will help!"

"What is going on here?" Valerie demanded.

"Tell her the truth, Father or I will!"

"Sara, what truth are you talking? You can tell me anything."

She broke into tears and exclaimed, "Everything you see here is a lie. It's all a big fat lie!"

Valerie's eyes widened.

"What are you talking about?" she asked in a controlled whisper.

The two glared at Garrison. He was used to witnessing fear in his daughter's eyes, but fear was no longer there. He knew the truth would be out, but opted for one last chance to bring back his scared little girl.

"Go ahead, Sara, tell your story," he dared.

If I have to, I'll accept the consequences, but I doubt she'll do it, he thought.

Sara's eyes lowered as she chittered out her bottom lip.

Garrison pressed his back against his seat and thought, *It's Lila. She has her mother's strength.* He swallowed hard. *I have no choice but to face the truth.*

"My father is a big phony! Ever since my mom left, he hasn't been here. All he does is drink and punish me." She hiccupped in a jagged breath and shouted, "I have to clean, cook and do everything before the monster attacks!"

Valerie leapt to her feet and pulled Sara to her side.

"Garrison—is this true?"

"Yes! It's true." He turned to Sara and added, "Are you happy now?"

Sara felt better hearing him admit the truth. She nodded, but when she thought she had stopped, the room continued shaking.

Valerie snagged her by the shoulders and lowered herself to Sara's eye level.

"Sara, please, calm down. I'm here and you'll be fine."

Something about Valerie's touch stopped the shakes from taking control. They did not completely stop, nor did they move to the next stage, which usually left her on the floor, violently shaking and unable to speak.

Once Valerie knew Sara had a little more control, she looked up at Garrison and demanded, "I want to know everything, and don't you dare lie to me."

At that exact moment, Sara felt as if the weight of world was off her shoulders.

Now we'll be free of the monster.

Sylvia Stein

Chapter Five

Valerie and Garrison sent Sara upstairs while they talked.

She knew the moment she was upstairs the truth would come out. She rushed into her room and waited for the monster to leave.

How will I know it's gone? Will the monster say goodbye? Aunt Valerie will know. She'll tell—

"Alright, Garrison," said Valerie, interrupting Sara's train of thought. "I'm all ears."

The thought of having to disclose the truth made Garrison nervous. His hands trembled as sweat beaded on his forehead.

In an attempt to buy time, he challenged, "What do you want to know?"

"The truth! Please, just tell me the truth.".

He knew that there was no running from what he had

done. Feeling helpless and ashamed, he gave in and told her everything.

Valerie could not believe her ears.

Valerie had learned how Sara spent most days taking care of him. Garrison admitted everything, including her fear of him. He said her fear gave him a sense of power. Something he had not felt since the day Lila was diagnosed with cancer..

"You mean to tell me Sara is the parent!"

"Yes," he admitted in a low whisper.

After taking a moment to collect her thoughts, Valerie snapped, "You mean t to tell me Sara is the parent while you bullied her into doing everything. You felt powerful? You, Garrison James, you are pathetic!"

"Garrison! You do realize Sara is only twelve?"

"I know how old my daughter is!"

Do you have any idea what you've done to her?"

"Valerie, please," he begged.

"No. I don't have to understand!"

"Look, losing Lila was hard, and I couldn't take the pain!"

"This is complete madness!" She leaned in and said, "What about Sara and her pain? You couldn't take it, your daughter needed you!"

"What about me?" Sara recognized his tone. Whenever Garrison used it, the monster soon followed. She could not sit idle with her aunt in danger.

If he returns, he'll hurt her!

She rushed into the hall and peered over the bannister. She needed to make sure Valerie was all right.

"Valerie—come on! I did the best I could. You have a husband, who do I have? No one. Even you left."

"You had a daughter. You better tell me everything or I'll call the police."

He knew she meant what she said. He opened up and told her everything, including his blackouts, Sara's secret hiding place that he had yet to find. Then he complimented Sara's cooking skills. He said it wasn't all bad because she learned how to cook and clean. He said those skills would help her in the real world.

For a brief moment, Valerie empathize with his pain. She knew how much Garrison loved her sister, but his actions were inexcusable.

"We all have pain," she coldly stated.

" Exactly," he replied.

However, he misunderstood her comments.

"You get it!"

"That is not what I meant!"

"Why are you mad at me? I'm telling you what losing you sister did to me."

It was too much for Valerie. She could not contain herself.

She shook her head in frustration.

"Are you kidding me?" She let out a sarcastic laugh.

"What?" he said.

"You are not the man I thought you were," she challenged.

She stormed forward and slapped him across the face.

He glared at her with tears in his eyes.

"Oh—please! You deserved that and so much more!" She took a deep breath and snarled, "You are a monster!"

Without waiting for a response, she stormed to the stairs and called out, "Sara, get your clothes and come down. You're coming home with me."

"Come on Sara."

She rushed around her room and stuffed as much as she could into her backpack. She did not want to leave her dad. She wanted the monster to leave.

Garrison feared she was taking Sara for good. If she did, he would be alone, and stuck knowing he had only himself to blame.

"How long is she visiting?" he asked.

"I'm taking her to live with me and Kyle. Do not fight this," she warned, "believe me, you will lose."

He dropped to his knees and begged, "Please don't! I don't want to be alone!"

She ignored him.

When Sara came down, Valerie guided her towards the door. "Don't worry, sweetheart, he'll never hurt you again."

As they walked out, Garrison stumbled to his feet and rushed to the doorway. He remained stoic and without any emotion until they were outside.

Closure

The truth was out in the open. He could not stop his tears. Although his tears were coupled with anger. He felt betrayed and blamed Sara for everything. She would never be able to forget the frown on her father's face.

"How could you betray me? You're my own flesh and blood!" he yelled.

Once they drove off, he slammed the door and stormed into the kitchen. He whipped the fridge open and pulled two bottles out. He opened them and downed the first, while taking a third bottle out and placing it on the counter. For the rest of the night, he continued to drink heavily.

A few hours and a dozen beers later, Garrison stumbled into the living room and flopped onto the couch.

"What is wrong with you?" he scolded himself.

His body tensed when he recalled Valerie's question, "What would Lila think?"

Knowing he disappointed Lila drove him over the edge. He pictured Valerie and Sara standing before him and began shouting, "Damn you both!"

The next morning, Garrison awoke in a pool of sweat. He noticed the blanketed odor of alcohol. He slowly got to his feet, stumbled to the mirror and glared at the reflection. He cringed at what he saw. This was one revelation he was not prepared to face. As he struggled to comprehend what he had become. The darkness swirled around him. He did not move or turn the light on. Instead, he wept.

What have I become? He wondered.

Chapter Six

Nearly six months had passed since Sara moved in with her Aunt and Uncle. They were residing in the city of Asheville, North Carolina.

The new surroundings were lovely. However, as nice as it all was for Sara, to her, home was back in Minnesota.

The new place felt distant and foreign. Sara could not help but feel insecure. She began clutching her chest and gasping for air.

"Sara, dear," said her Aunt.

She looked away from her Aunt.

"Please, look at me."

After a few minutes, she gave in and made eye contact.

"I know this is all new and you are still getting used to things, but give it a chance. We hope you will be happy here with us." Valerie smiled.

Sara began to relax and started to arch her neck back on the kitchen chair. It was a feeling she had not felt since her mother's passing. For the first, time she felt good and smiled back to her Aunt.

The past continued to haunt her, usually through nightmares. She often woke soaked in sweat and begging for forgiveness. Sara needed the nightmares to end but did not know how to stop them.

Grateful for her new life, she longed for her nights to mirror her days. Sara could not understand why she was haunted. She had what she thought was lost forever. Love, understanding, and a real home. She could finally enjoy life, instead of cleaning up after a drunken, aggressive monster.

Still, she felt guilty. At her young age, she could not help but think of her father. In Sara's eyes, her dad was innocent. It was the monster inside him who destroyed their lives.

She never meant to hurt her father. All she ever wanted was him to love her like she loved him.

One night, Sara woke terrified. She snuck downstairs and poured herself a glass of water.

Fearful of the monster on the couch, she bolted out the backdoor and sought refuge in a large barn that belonged to her aunt and uncle.

It worked.

She slept peacefully the rest of the night. Soon, it became a habit.

One morning, Sara did not return before they woke.

Closure

They feared Garrison found them and took her during the night.

Her aunt ran into the kitchen to call the police, as she brought the phone to her ear, she noticed the barn door was wide open, and heard the horses making strange sounds.

She dropped the phone and bolted out the backdoor with Kyle on her heels. There, they found Sara sleeping in the barn.

They tried to follow the doctor's advice and give her the space she needed. It did not seem to work. Feeling helpless, they needed to understand what was happening. They questioned her, which made Sara feel overwhelmed and confused. Valerie and Kyle were lost. Finding a child in the barn worried them. They needed to know what they could do.

Valerie decided that confronting Sara was best.

"Sara, sweetie, we know you've been through a lot. Uncle Kyle and I are concerned, and we think it would be beneficial for you to speak with a new doctor about everything your father and you have been through."

Sara paused for a moment. She was nervous. After considering their feelings, she said, "Are you talking about a new shrink?" Before they could answer, her hands began to shake as she gasped for air.

"Don't panic," pleaded Val.

"You think they can help me?"

"I think we should check it out," reassured her Uncle Kyle.

"Will my nightmares ever stop?"

Kyle gave a slow nod and said, "Not right away, but I am sure this doctor will help."

"I am just not ready," she said.

Sara felt uneasy with the idea of talking to another stranger, and having to relive the painful memories from her past. She wanted to be free of her nightmares, but she feared the cost. Just then, a more determined look crossed over her face as she decided to accept the offer.

"If this is the key to getting better, I'll do it."

She could see her decision made her Aunt and Uncle happy. They smiled and pulled her into a tight hug.

Later that night, she felt anxious and was not able to sleep. She walked across her room, looked out the window and tried to breathe in the fresh air.

Without warning, she fell to the ground and grasped her chest.

Is it going to explode?

She was too young to understand what was happening.

For minutes, all she could do was lay there and think about her mother.

Oh mama, I am here.

Sara was pulled away from her thoughts when she heard her name in a hysterical scream.

"Sara! Sara!" Val shouted, "Quick, Kyle call an ambulance!"

Closure

Terrified and breathless, she closed her eyes and fought to ask for help.

"Don't worry, sweetie, help is on its way," Val said while stroking Sara's hair away from her face.

Chapter Seven

The ride to the hospital seemed endless. Sara could not understand what was happening.

She tried not to panic when she began feeling a deep pressure in her chest. It was an indication that another attack would strike. She knew that feeling was followed by another shake attack. She tried her best to not panic, but was terrified of those shakes.

Her mind screamed, *I need to hide!*

"It is okay, now, Sara. Take a deep breath," called a woman's voice.

She did her best to follow instructions.

It seemed to work.

"Very good," said a nurse. She gave a soothing smile before writing in a chart.

"What happened?" asked Sara.

"You had a seizure. We brought you to the hospital to make sure everything is okay," chimed her Aunt Valerie.

Closure

When she heard her aunt's voice, she let out a sigh of relief, and smiled. She felt a little safer.

"When will I be able to go home?"

"Soon—we are just waiting for the doctor to come and see us."

All of a sudden, Sara felt agitated and began shaking again. Her mind was all over the place. After all, hospitals were not her favorite place.

She began to kick and scream.

"Sara, honey, what is wrong?"

"I don't want to see a doctor!"

Just then, Sara began to have a flashback of her mother in and out of the hospital. She was too weak to get up.

She looked up and saw doctors and nurses pool in the hall.

Valerie turned in the direction Sara was glaring. It reminded her of Lila's many hospital trips. She turned to Sara and asked, "Are you thinking of your mother?"

"Yes! Mama died in a hospital."

After a short pause, Valerie walked over to her niece and gave her a hug.

"I promise it will be okay."

"Doctors are the enemy! You can't trust them."

"Please, don't worry. It will be okay. Besides—the type of doctor you are going to see is a psychiatrist."

"Wait. I have heard of those. Does this mean I'm crazy?"

"No. Darlin', you're not crazy," she said with an assuring smile.

"Then why are they coming to see me?"

"Well—you had a type of seizure. They believe it was caused by anxiety, and, well, after talking with the nurses and the ER doctor on staff. They recommended it."

"Nothing has been confirmed yet," said a man.

Sara recognized the voice. She shot up into a seated position and peered around Valerie.

"Uncle Kyle!"

"Hi," he said with a deep chuckle, "I thought I would come and check in on my girls."

"Thank you," Sara squeaked. She loved her uncle Kyle. He was fun.

Valerie was also happy to see Kyle. With everything that had happened to Sara, she was glad to have him there to help.

Valerie noticed that Sara was getting sleepy. She signaled Kyle to walk out the door so they could speak to the nurses in private.

It was not easy for Sara to admit she had a problem. It made her feel helpless. She was hoping they would let her go.

Sadly, it was not the case. Once the appointment was set to see the psychiatrist, Sara felt nervous. She pictured the psychiatrist sending her to a mental ward. Forcing her to take pills, and taking her away from the only family she had left. All those possibilities weighed heavily on her. She began feeling dizzy and lightheaded.

Closure

She felt guilty for leaving her father alone with the monster.

Both her aunt and uncle wanted their niece to get the best care possible, and they knew it would be the first step towards her having a normal childhood.

Valerie sent Kyle to the nurse's station to set the appointment while she took a moment to have a one-on-one with Sara. She marched into the room and carefully sat on the side of Sara's bed.

As she gently took Sara's hand, she said, "I realize that going to see a psychiatrist can seem overwhelming, but it will all be alright."

"I am not sure about that, Aunt Valerie!"

"Please, listen to me," pleaded her aunt.

Hesitantly, Sara turned her head and slowly looked up at her aunt.

"I know you are scared, honey."

She yanked her hand away and crossed her arms over her chest.

"I'm not sure about that."

Valerie placed a hand on Sara's shoulder. She noted whenever she touched her, Sara relaxed and was able to maintain control.

"Sweetie, hear me out."

Sara locked eyes and tried to move away.

Valerie could see her panic and pressed her back.

"I'm scared!"

"It is all going to work out," Valerie said in a soothing tone.

"I don't want to talk with strangers! Not about that."

"I promise . . . this is going to help you so much, darlin'."

"I'm not sure." Sara tried not to show her fear but she could not help it. "I can't do this." Sara began biting her bottom lip to try and stop it from trembling.

Valerie realized the extent of Sara's abuse. She did not want to make it harder than it had to be.

"Sara, please. We know what's best."

After a few minutes, which seemed as if it had lasted for hours, Sara began to calm down.

"Honey, I know it feels as if I'm pressuring you, and maybe I am, but it's because I want the best for you. What you've been through is not normal. The doctor will help you move past it."

"Are you sure?"

"I am confident, and together, we'll get through this. We'll take it one step at a time."

Something about Valerie's words made her feel safe.

After a moment, she gave a firm nod and said, "We'll do it."

The next few minutes slowly passed. Each time a doctor or nurse walked by, Valerie noticed Sara would flinch or begin to tremble.

Guilt began to sink in.

Valerie reconsidered the psychiatrist. She was about to

get up to cancel the appointment when Sara sat up and pulled her aunt into a hug.

She felt Sara's body relax against hers, and whispered, "Together, we'll get through this."

Chapter Eight

After several months of living in a drunken stupor, Garrison woke to a loud pounding sound. His head felt as if it was about to explode.

Enraged by the noise, he shouted, "What?"

He stumbled to his feet and staggered towards the source. He whipped the front door open.

There stood a young girl wearing a scout uniform and holding cookies.

Her nose crinkled as she backed away whispering, "Sorry."

The young girl did not give him a chance to reply. Instead, she ran as fast as she could to the sidewalk.

He slammed the door and stormed into the living room, as he brought the near empty bottle to his lips, he caught his reflection in the mirror housed above the fireplace.

Shame engulfed him, which quickly turned to rage.

Garrison looked at the bottle and snarled, "It's your

fault. You took everything from me." He whipped the bottle across the room. "Never again!"

It was at that moment, he made the bold decision to quit drinking.

After seeing the look the young girl gave him, he immediately thought of Sara. He decided he wanted his life back.

That was the day Garrison began a journey to try to get sober. He knew it would not be an easy road, but after the big confrontation with Valerie, and having Sara witness it, he wanted to try to better himself.

There is no turning back, his mind stated as he searched the local directory for assistance.

It was then that he recalled his friend talking about meetings he attended at the local Y.M.C.A.

That's what I'll do!

After getting all the information from the director, he was ready.

Two days later, he nervously got dressed. His mind raced with different scenarios. He worried about how they would judge him, what they would say, and what they might think of him.

"This is the only way to make it better and try to salvage your relationship with Sara," he whispered.

Just then, tears began to overtake him.

The meeting was a short block away from his house.

He decided to walk. Even though, the weather was chilly.

His thoughts turned to Sara.

Then he did something that he had not done in years.

He began to pray.

"Lord, I know it has been awhile, but I really want to get sober. I know I have so much work ahead of me. Please, give me the strength to stick through this, to battle my demons, and to become a better man and father."

He continued repeating his prayers until he was in front of the building. Before opening the door, he wiped his tears away.

When was the last time I was around people? he wondered.

The more he thought about it, the more he realized his mistakes

"Everyone," he mumbled in amazement. "I pushed everyone away. Even my own daughter doesn't want to be near me. I don't blame her. I chose the bottle over her. I broke her heart."

Engulfed in his personal argument, he was caught by surprise when one of the people at the meeting approached him.

"Please, friend, come and join us," said a tall, bearded man.

"Oh—thank you."

"The meeting will begin in about fifteen minutes. In the meantime, you can help yourself to some coffee and donuts bought by our group. "By the way," he added, "you can call me Thomas."

Garrison nodded and replied, "Thanks, it's nice to meet you."

As the time got closer, Garrison's heart raced and his palms filled with sweat. For a split second, he considered walking out.

However, as he listened to the different members share their own stories of what had brought them there, Garrison began to envision Sara coming home. The images flickered through his mind. He was determined to stay and get the help he needed. As the meeting began wrapping up, he began to feel he was on the right path.

This brought a small smile to his face.

Finally. I'm doing something right.

Chapter Nine

The next two years passed by rather quickly. Sara was growing into a beautiful woman. She had changed, very different from the young, frail girl of twelve that had come to live in Asheville.

Sara was now fourteen years old. She looked more like her mother, and had the similar love for cooking. She enjoyed creating new recipes the same way Lila had.

Valerie stood in the hall and watched Sara at the kitchen counter humming and stirring a whisk in a large bowl.

Everyday she looks more and more like Lila. Except her eyes, I wonder where she got those piercing blue eyes? She instantly recalled the day Lila introduced her to Garrison. *That's right, she has Garrison's eyes. His eyes changed . . . he's changed. When I look at Sara, I see a young, innocent angel. I don't understand any of this. How could he hurt her? Why would he hurt his only family?*

Closure

Valerie continued to worry, she knew her niece was not sleeping well.

Since the hospital, Sara made some progress, but she also had many set backs. The psychologist they sent her to wanted to medicate her. He said she would be fine with the right medication, patience, and a little space.

Sara's nightmares continued to haunt her, and her panic attacks grew more intense. She wondered if they would ever stop and wanted to talk about it, but felt ashamed and embarrassed. The last thing she wanted to do was disappoint her aunt and uncle.

They spent a lot of money and time trying to help me. That doctor said they'd go away or ease up when I got older? Maybe I should tell them and stop hiding them. They should know.

She reached to her right for a half cup of sugar and saw Valerie in her peripheral. While adding the sugar she fought back her giggle.

Aunt Val may not be a great cook, but she loves watching and learning. Now's the time, I'll tell her everything.

She placed the empty measuring cup into the sink and turned to face her aunt. Valerie was no longer in the hall. Sara immediately lost her nerve.

Tomorrow, I'll sit down and tell them everything tomorrow.

That night, Sara had an intense nightmare.

She screamed so loud it woke the entire house.

Kyle leapt out of bed and was about to head into Sara's room, but Valerie stopped him and reminded him of the doctor's advice.

"Wait thirty seconds. If the screams continue then go in," she whispered. "We'll have a family meeting in the morning."

"I think that doctor is a quack," Kyle muttered. "He said to give her space, her father ignored her."

"Yes, and that's why we need to give her space. We don't want her to feel smothered."

The next day, Valerie and Kyle were waiting in the kitchen for Sara to wake. Kyle paced while Valerie cradled her tea. Neither knew how to begin the discussion.

When Sara woke, she decided to tell them the truth. With determination, she walked into the kitchen, sat down and told them everything that happened over the past two years. The nightmares, the attacks she had in her room and the ones at school.

Once she began, she could not stop. She even told them how the other kids act whenever she is near, and how she felt about herself.

Together, they decided the treatment she had was not working. Kyle suggested a new doctor, one with less patients or better credentials.

Sara agreed.

Nobody was happier than Valerie.

On the day of her appointment, Sara's heart began to race uncontrollably.

Valerie noticed.

"It is all going to work out, honey."

"I hope so," Sara said while trying to remain optimistic.

Val reached out and placed a hand on her Sara's shoulder.

"Dr. Anne Baker comes highly recommended, and I promise, things will be alright."

Wanting her aunt to feel more at ease, she gave a confident nod and said, "I'm taking your advice, I'm going to be open-minded and try to trust this doctor."

I hope it all works out she deserves happiness, thought Valerie.

Dr. Anne Baker was a qualified psychologist who had graduated at the top of her class at John Hopkins School of Medicine in Baltimore, Maryland. She had a specialty in child and adolescent medicine and psychology. She was going on her 18th year, and was as dedicated to her work as the first day she began. Doctor Baker never married and did not have children. All of her energy went to her career.

Once inside, Sara noticed all the awards that covered most of the walls. While waiting her turn, she began reading each award.

She heard her name called out. She turned and saw a tall, slender woman smiling at her.

"Good morning. Are you Dr. Anne Baker? I have an appointment to see her."

"Yes, I am. Please, come in. Are you Miss. James?"

Sara paused for a moment before replying, "Yes, and you're Dr. Baker."

The doctor gave an assuring smile. "I see you are familiar with me."

"Yes, sort of." Her eyes danced between the doctor and the wall. "Only what I've read on the walls."

Dr. Baker laughed and said, "It is nice to finally meet you Miss. James."

"I am glad to be here."

I think.

"The pleasure is all mine, Miss. James," said the doctor.

"Thank you, but you can just call me Sara."

"Sara it is."

The gesture of addressing her by her first name pleased Dr. Baker. It was an early indication of trust.

While waiting for the doctor to begin her session, Sara began to fidget in her seat.

Dr. Baker noticed. She decided to give Sara control. Instead of telling her what she knew, she wanted Sara to openly state it.

"Using your own words, tell me why you are here and what your expectations are with me?"

Sara began to feel uncomfortable and out of breath.

"Sara it is okay." The doctor gave an assuring smile.

"I just—I don't even know how to begin."

"Tell me about yourself. What do you like to do in your spare time?"

Sara felt another panic attack coming on. She did not know how to stop it. She tried to take in a breath but could not do it. Each time she inhaled, her chest tightened, she would exhale and try again. Soon, she was hiccupping in small gulps of air.

She is showing signs of a panic attack and not a seizure. Possibly a misdiagnosis, both have similar symptoms.

Dr. Baker took the initiative and began to speak to her in a soft tone of voice.

"Sara, take a deep breath."

Trusting another adult seemed impossible for Sara, but Dr. Baker was different. Her voice and tone caught her attention.

"Relax your muscles and take a deep breath," the doctor repeated.

Sara focused on the doctor's lips and read each word. Soon, the attack was under control.

Wow, she thought, as her attack faded away.

Once it was completely gone, Dr. Baker got up and poured Sara a glass of water. She held it out to her and said, "When you're ready, tell me about yourself."

After taking a small sip, Sara shrugged and said, "There's not much to tell. I was born and raised in Minneapolis, Minnesota. My parents are Garrison and Lila James."

"What can you tell me about your parents?"

Sara took a long pause before replying.

"My mom was amazing."

Baker waited for more but Sara said nothing.

"And your father?"

Sara ignored her and focused on a piece of fluff she saw on her jeans.

The doctor knew the signs of abuse. Sara was evading questions about her father.

Baker tried again.

"Your mother sounds lovely. What about your father? What can you tell me about him?

Rage boiled in the pit of Sara's stomach. She slowly shook her head and said, "Nothing good."

"I didn't ask for good or bad. I asked what can you, Sara, tell me about your father?"

Memories of her running out of the house and into the barn raced through her mind. The monster was angry and after her.

She glared at the doctor and said, "He's a mean drunk who didn't give a damn about me." She plunked forward and buried her face in her hands. "My mother was the best mother ever, but she died because of cancer!"

"I imagine it was not easy for you," said the doctor.

Insulted by the doctors words, she snapped, "No—it clearly wasn't!"

"How old where you when she passed?"

"I was only four, well, four and a half, almost five."

Dr. Baker could see her struggle, but knew if she cut the appointment short it might cause more damage. She decided to address the real problem.

"Tell me about your father, Garrison. I can imagine your mother's death was hard on him as well."

Hearing his name made her angry. She wanted to

scream and run out of the office but knew her aunt would force her back in.

She snapped, "I don't want to talk about him!"

"Why is that?"

"Because he was a monster! He . . . he..."

She fought to find the words.

The good doctor knew she could not let Sara stop. If she did, she might lose her trust.

"Your mother married a monster?" she asked.

"No! After my mother died the monster came into our lives!"

Sara took in a deep breath and let out a heavy sigh of relief.

The doctor could see a huge weight lifted of Sara's shoulders. She decided that was enough for their first meeting. The moment Sara looked up at her, she smiled and said, "Alright, Sara, I think our session is over."

Confused by her words, Sara asked, "So that's it? We're done?"

"For today we are. We will meet twice a week."

"Twice a week. For what?"

"For our therapy sessions."

"Oh, but why? I'm not cured?" asked Sara.

"Not Yet, Sara, but this is good start."

"Then . . . then I guess I'll see you next time?"

"Yes, you will, and I promise, in time, things will get better."

Unsure about the meeting, Sara began second-guessing her aunt recommending Dr. Baker.

"I sure hope this helps," she mumbled under her breath as she left the building.

Inside the office, Baker began her notes. She decided to dictate them into a recorder.

"The patient, Sara James, is a young woman holding onto pain from her childhood. She lost her mother, Lila James, months before her fifth birthday. Although this was our first meeting, the patient clearly blames her father, Garrison James. She displays great resentment when hearing her father's name. It is my hope to be able to get her to share more in each session. Patient suffers from panic-attacks, which stopped once the patient focused on her breathing and opened up. Medicinal assistance will be decided at a later date."

Chapter Ten

For Sara, acknowledging she had a problem was the first step in the right direction. As the sessions continued, Sara began addressing her issues more openly. Dr. Baker had gained her trust and respect, and Sara knew she was safe.

Even though it was hard to talk about her past, she was able to take it all in stride.

Soon after, her sleep became easier and the nightmares were less frequent. Sara began to look forward to her appointments.

"I must admit I could not be more pleased with your progress."

"I am trying to take it one day at a time," replied a calmer Sara.

The progress also helped Sara at school. She seemed to be more in control of her emotions, and was no longer having to leave early in fear of having an attack during class.

At home, there were moments when Sara would give up and lash out at Valerie. She accused her of choosing the wrong doctor and wanted to stop going.

Valerie began to wonder if the therapy was a good idea. She worried for her niece and feared she made the wrong choice.

What if I'm not helping her? What if the sessions are hurting her? It's all my fault.

Luckily, Dr. Baker was able to reassure Sara's family that all was going well.

"Believe me, I have seen and heard it all. Every case is different, but I promise you, Sara is going to be fine. She locked a lot of her pain inside, once it's out, she will begin to heal."

The doctor's words were soothing for Sara's aunt and uncle. They knew that this was a step in the right direction, no matter how tormented the road was to get her through it.

Baker expected a call from Sara's family due to the more intense sessions.

During the heated sessions, both Baker and Sara would take a moment to collect themselves. Sara needed to control her emotions and Baker needed to build her professional wall. She cared about all her patients, but Sara was different. Somehow, she broke through the wall and made it into Baker's heart.

It confused the doctor. After all, she had her share of difficult cases before, but the combination of mental and physical abuse, mixed with alcohol induced rage and the mourning of loving parent, made it more of an excruciating path.

On the day Valerie called the doctor, Sara had an emotional session. Each time the doctor mentioned Garrison's name, Sara would change the subject. The doctor was strong, and redirected her questions.

"Why do we have to talk about him?" Sara practically shouted.

"Like it or not, Sara, your father is the center of your problems. It is important that we talk about him."

"Fine," snapped Sara. She crossed her arms and flopped back in the chair. "Garrison James seemed like a good man and father. He owned a farm, had his own stable, and ran a construction company. He and my mother were high school sweethearts."

"I already know that. Can you tell me something new? What did you used to do together as a family?"

Just then, Sara's face had a sudden glow.

"We use to horseback ride."

Baker was impressed with Sara's openness. She noticed Sara was exceptionally touchy that day. The doctor leaned forward and said, "Tell me more. I love horses. It's been years since I've ridden one. Tell me more about your rides."

"I don't remember much. I know my mom used to love riding. Aunt Val said we went every Saturday and my mom would always pack a picnic lunch for us."

"You are from Minnesota. Did you have cold winters there?"

"Yeah, we did. But I was talking about riding in the summer. Our summers were hot."

"Well that sounds like fun."

"It was. My mom told us to keep doing them, but we didn't."

"Why didn't you?"

Sara's jaw clenched.

"Because he didn't care. He hated me and loved the bottle."

Dr. Baker realized Sara beginning to hyperventilate. It seemed to happen whenever she lashed out at her father.

"Sara, take it easy," said the doctor in a calmer tone.

"No! Doc, I just can't do this. I can't pretend he cared."

It was at this time Dr. Baker realized Sara was angry and not having an attack. She knew she couldn't stop the session, Sara's anger would help her say what she's feeling.

"Sara, are you angry?"

"Yes I am," she snapped.

"Okay, so, who are you angry at?"

Sara's mind raced.

"Don't think," said Baker. "Say the first thing that comes to mind."

"I am angry at how the alcohol changed him."

Sara began crying.

"Okay. Do you blame the drinking?"

Her neck snapped up as she growled, "Yes, I do!"

The doctor gave her a nod of approval.

"This is a good thing."

Surprised by her response, Sara asked, "What do you mean?"

"When you first arrived, you used to blame yourself. You didn't clean enough. You didn't cook the food right. You didn't feed the animals, and you constantly said you were a bad daughter. Now, you realize that it wasn't you. Your father had an illness, he was an alcoholic, and unfortunately—his illness fogged reality. He did not see his daughter or life the way a healthy parent would. Sara, these sessions are working, and you are able to see that you are not at fault. Now that you see it, you can move forward and begin healing. Maybe, in time, you will consider talking with him. Give him a call and see how he's doing."

After a long moment of thought, Sara shrugged and said, "Maybe, but not today."

"That's fair and mature of you. You are growing into a responsible adult."

Those words made Sara think of her mother, Lila.

"My mother used to tell me how mature I was for my age."

"I am so glad to hear you say that, Sara."

Dr. Baker learned that Sara respected honesty. She decided to be frank with her. "I can tell you that even though it has not been an easy road, everything, including sleep will get better."

"I sure hope so."

"Remember, time heals all wounds."

Nonetheless, the issues surrounding the abuse Garrison did was more of a work in progress. Dr. Baker knew it would take a lot of time, but Sara was strong and would get through it.

Later that evening, Dr. Baker took time to collaborate with her colleagues. From the beginning, she felt Sara's case was special, and needed some insight. One of her closest confidants was Dr. Charles Malloy.

They opted to have a conference call.

During the call, Baker tried to hide the fact she was emotionally attached to Sara. She wanted to get a second opinion without disclosing her patient's name.

In the meantime, Dr. Malloy asked Dr. Baker to write a thesis and paper, since he was doing a study on abused children and their parents. In return, he promised to add it to the study manuals and curriculum for the annual psychologist journal of medicine. Baker agreed.

As the years moved on, Sara continued to open up. When she became a senior in high school and neared commencement, she pondered what her future would be. She was uncertain what type of career she would like to have, and if her father would be a part of it.

Chapter Eleven

December 1999

Dear Diary,

Doc tells me to write about my feelings. How do I feel? Am I angry? And to tell you the truth, I'm very confused and don't know what to say.

There is something that worries me. Almost every night, I wake up and want to run and hide in the barn, the same way I did when I was a kid. I don't know how to make this stop. It always happens in middle of the night, and I cannot seem to go back to sleep.

Gosh, I am so stupid! Here I am away from the monster that destroyed my life, and for some reason, I feel as if he has a hold on me.

I need to forget about all he had done, but I can't. I'm afraid I will never be able to move on. To live the life I want to live.

What am I holding onto? Why and I holding onto it? I don't owe the monster or my father anything. He didn't care about me.

Chapter Eleven

But why do I feel guilty for him? Why guilt? I am so angry at the way he makes me feel.

It's because of him I'll never be normal. Everyday I feel as if I want to hide. My anxiety rises, and then I feel trapped.

I wish I could make all of this just go away. But I can't. The scars that I have to deal with are eating me up, and I do not think I will ever be free of the pain that I feel. I am tired of lying to others and saying I'm okay when I'm not.

~Sara

Chapter Twelve

Garrison seemed to be making progress. He was attending weekly A.A. meetings at the local Y.M.C.A.

Speaking out helped, but he knew there would be more to come. This feeling of telling his story really terrified him.

It was not easy for him to let himself become vulnerable and admit his guilt. He remained hopeful as he continued to carry out the twelve steps to his sobriety, which he read each day as he walked into the building.

Garrison understood that fear was not an option and that he had to try his best. Upon entering, he bowed his head and prayed.

"Lord, give me the strength," he pleaded.

When he finished his prayer, he looked up and read each step.

He focused on step number five and read it aloud, "Admitted to God, to ourselves, and to another human being the exact nature of our wrongs. Don't worry number five, I will."

Chapter Twelve

With step five fresh on his mind, Garrison decided to go first.

He marched to the front of the room and said, "My name is Garrison James, and I am an alcoholic." The moment he said those words, his tears began to flow. He closed his eyes and tried to control his emotions.

Flashes of his past took over.

The silence in the room consumed everyone.

Using the sleeve of his shirt, he wiped his tears away and began sharing his story.

He began with the day he and his wife listened to the doctor's diagnosis. How he kissed his daughter goodnight, and laid beside his wife until she fell into a deep sleep. He explained his quiet trip to the barn, and told them that was where he secretly drank a bottle of wine, while crying in the darkness beside the horses.

He opened up and explained how each sip from a single bottle took away the bitter anger he had towards the doctor and God. How that bottle helped him sleep. He felt sleep was his only escape from the harsh reality of life.

Once he finished his story, he brought his hand to his chest as he said with confidence, "I have no one to blame but myself. I have not seen my daughter in a long time, and my only hope is that she forgives me—one day."

At that moment, Garrison felt a sense of purpose. He decided his only priority was to live each day clean and sober. He would do everything in his power to build a relationship with Sara.

Chapter Twelve

Members clapped.

He remained calm and focused on what he wanted to say.

"A few years ago, if anyone asked me if I would consider an AA meeting, I would have laughed it off," he said. He paused when he heard a slight tremble in his tone. "I am here because I am an alcoholic, and I came to get help. Please help me become a better person, so I can have a relationship with my daughter." He stopped to catch his breath before adding, "My addiction started when I lost my beloved wife—she was my—my everything. When she died, a part of me died with her."

Garrison took a pause as he recalled when Lila began fighting the cancer.

He opened up and shared how strong his wife was inside while on the outside she became frail. How the color began to fade from her face. Her cries in the middle of the night, the pain she suffered, and the many times she was sick due to the chemotherapy. It was unbearable. He wanted was to escape. He admitted how his first drink did exactly that, or so he thought.

When he finished, one of the sponsors got up and stood beside him. He gently placed his hands on Garrison's back and said, "This is the first step. It will get better, my friend."

"I can only hope," mumbled Garrison.

"Have faith my friend."

"I'm trying, but..."

Chapter Twelve

"Believe me, friend, making blame will not fix things. You have a goal, a reason to get better, and new friends." He waves his hand out towards the group. "We have all been right where you are today. You are taking the steps, and as long as you take them one at a time, you will reach your destination."

Feeling slightly overwhelmed by the sponsors wise response, he let out a heavy sigh and said, "Thank you, but . . . what if I . . . you see . . . I couldn't handle watching my wife suffer with the pain. The bottle was easier than the truth." He locked eyes with the sponsor and blurted, "I was a coward! What if I still am? What if my daughter rejects me? What if—instead of proving I can be better, I go back to the bottle?"

"Look, friend, there is no guarantee. It will not be easy, but we are here." He patted Garrison's shoulder. "When you feel the bottle is calling you, call your sponsor. Your sponsor will help keep you strong."

"Thank you," whispered Garrison. He felt better knowing he was not the only one who heard the bottles calling.

When he stepped to take a seat, he heard other people in the meeting shout words of encouragement.

"We are here for you."

"Don't give up, brother."

"Stand strong."

It was the first time he felt like himself. He knew it was

not going to be an easy road, but for the first time in a long time, Garrison felt there was a possibility for a better life.

Back in Asheville, Sara was having a difficult session with Dr. Baker.

She sat back and began talking about her mother's death.

Each time, the doctor redirected the questions from her mother to her father.

"Why must you always bring him up?" she screamed.

"We have been through this. In order to help you, we have to talk about him. "

"Fine," snapped Sara.

She clenched her chest.

Baker noticed.

"I know this is hard, so take a deep breath."

"Why do you insist on making me remember him?"

"Your father is the root, not your mother."

"Fine . . . whatever."

Baker smiled at Sara's normal teenage response.

"So, your father, do you feel he is to blame?"

Suddenly, Sara began to picture the closet she would hide in when the monster was loose. She closed her eyes and began to tremble.

Dr. Baker observed her demeanor.

"Are you okay?"

Then within a few moments Sara snarled, "I'm fine."

Very good, she is recognizing and controlling her panic

attacks. Maintain control, and remember to treat Sara like any other patient.

"Do you blame your father?"

"Yes, I blame him!" She pouted.

During the session, Dr. Baker learned more about Sara's underlying anger than in all her other sessions combined.

"I don't want to talk about him. Can we talk about something, anything else?"

"No. Your father is the root, Sara. We have to talk about him?"

"I would much rather speak about my mother."

"We'll compromise and talk about both. How about that?"

Sara nodded.

"What else can you share about your mother?"

"My mother was such a wonderful person, who was also an amazing cook." Sara pictured her mother's recipe catalogue and smiled.

"How was she amazing and wonderful? Do you remember specific things?"

"In so many ways! She knew how to cook just about everything, and I was always eager to learn. There are so many pictures of me in the kitchen helping her."

"I can tell you shared a wonderful bond with your mother."

"Yes, she was the best."

"So, tell me, did you ever share any of these moments with your father?"

Chapter Twelve

"No! No! No!" Sara screamed, "He ruined everything!"

Dr. Baker tried not to get discouraged. Even though, each time they got close to a breakthrough, her patient would lose control.

"Take a deep breath."

"No! I think it is time for me to go."

"Sara, look at me."

"What is it now, Doc?" she cried.

Seeing how distraught Sara became, Dr. Baker handed her some tissues.

"I agree, I think it is time we stop for the day."

"Thanks, Doc."

Chapter Thirteen

Three years had passed. Sara was seventeen and Garrison seemed to be on the right track. He was working towards getting his life back to normal.

He completed all but the fifth step.

Whenever he tried to reach out to Sara, Valerie or Kyle would answer the phone. Before he could explain his sobriety, they would cut him off and hang up.

I have to try. I won't let them hang up without hearing how long I've been clean.

As he brought the phone to his ear, his mind warned, *Be ready, if it's Kyle, I won't have a chance to say a word. Dear, God, I hope Valerie answers.*

On the fourth ring, Valerie answered the phone.

Thank you!

"Hi, Valerie, it's Garrison."

Silence followed.

Maybe it's Sara!

"Hello? Are . . . are you there?" he whispered in a near stutter.

Chapter Thirteen

"Garrison, don't call here again," Valerie said with warning.

"I just want to know how my daughter is doing!"

"Sorry, but you lost the right to know about her a long time ago!"

A loud click followed.

"Dammit," he muttered while placing the phone on its receiver.

Feeling frustrated and hurt, he sat down and looked over the list his sponsor helped him create. Whenever he felt down or wanted a drink, he would read his list. Sara was his number one goal, and he desperately wanted to mend things with her.

"They said it would be a hard road, but how do I show them when they won't let me say a word?"

Below Sara's name was a list of the things he lost during his drunken years.

"Church, working on the farm, some of our horses, and the construction company," he read aloud.

He was grateful for his reconnection with his old church.

The farm was doing well, but it had been years since he enjoyed a ride or worked on it.

He was fortunate to have the young boy name Mitch help with the horses. The boy's father and Garrison made an agreement. Instead of paying money, Garrison gave him a horse. Mitch continued to care for all the horses, and in return for service, he did not have to pay vet or stable fees.

Chapter Thirteen

He lightly underlined the word farm and said, "That's what I'll do. Instead of paying others, I'll start working on the farm as well."

With optimism, he quickly stood to get his boots.

Unexplainable pain shot into his back. He stood frozen in place and waited till the pain died down. "I must have pulled a muscle," he mumbled to himself.

One day, the pain became unbearable and he decided to consult his doctor.

After a few routine exams, he was asked to come back so that his doctor could go over the results with him.

Garrison expected this visit to be nothing serious. He was taken back when the doctor informed him they had found a mass, they conducted some tests which confirmed it was cancer.

The news left Garrison in disbelief.

How can this be happening now! OH. Not now!

Garrison wanted to scream. Cancer was not something he expected to hear about again. After all, it had taken his beloved wife Lila away and then he began his long spiral of alcohol which led to the neglect and abuse of his only daughter Sara.

I will beat this! I will!

He was told he had to start chemotherapy right away.

"Lord, help me get better. I want to have a chance with my daughter," he pleaded

Flooded with countless emotions, he decided to go to church and pray.

"Lord, help me to stay on the wagon. Help me to fight the urge to drink, and, please, help me to beat this cancer."

The one thing that kept plaguing into his head was if he should let Sara know of his condition, or earn her trust and then tell her.

He decided he would not give up. He thought of his wife. How she faced and fought cancer, and decided that was what he would do. He knew he had to try.

For an entire week, each morning, he stood in front of the mirror and weighed his options.

He decided he would not share his illness with anyone. He wanted Sara to see the man he had become, and remember father he used to be, before he chose the bottle.

"I don't want her to see a dying man or an abusive drunk," he said to his reflection. "No . . . she needs to see and know I'm better for her. I don't want her to think cancer changed me. It wasn't the cancer. Losing my baby made me want to change."

Chapter Fourteen

A week before Sara's graduation, Valerie noticed her moving throughout the kitchen. She could not believe her eyes.

Her moves are nearly identical to Lila's.

When Sara expressed her joy in creating a new recipe, Valerie decided to share her thoughts.

"Honey, when your mother and I were growing up we used to share our goals and dreams with each other. Did you know you mother wanted to be a professional chef?"

"Really?" Sara asked while pulling a chair out and taking a seat.

Valerie joined her at the table.

"Yes. She really did. I hope— no." She paused before continuing. "I think you should consider culinary school."

"Do you think I have what it takes?"

"I honestly do," Valerie replied with confidence. "I must admit, seeing your love for the kitchen brings back fond memories of Lila." She chuckled and admitted, "Some not so tasty experiments. I was your mother's Guiney Pig." She sighed. "But all were fond memories."

Lost for words, Sara hopped out of the chair and hugged her aunt.

"Okay you two, it is time to get ready for dinner," said Kyle.

Sara and her aunt broke into laugher.

The day Sara had worried about was nearly upon her. For most teens her age, graduation should have been an exciting time. Not to say she was unhappy. She was confused.

Sara was shy and had difficulty making friends her own age. She seemed to relate best with her aunt, uncle, and Dr. Baker.

She wanted to be normal, but her seizures made her a pariah. Her peers did not understand her, and Sara did not know how or what she could do to seem normal. She tried her best to hide her seizures, but there were times they snuck up on her before she had a chance to get away from the other students.

The glares were what bothered her most.

Sara did not like when others looked at her with sympathy, or the ones whose eyes widened when she sat beside them on the bus or in class.

She heard the whispers and remarks.

There were times when the whispers caused her to feel anxious. Soon she was battling for control. Terrified the student would hear her controlled breathing and call more attention to her.

The night before graduation, Sara began to feel distressed.

She went online and watched videos of other graduations. She wanted to see what was expected and how to behave.

"I don't want to be the freak anymore," she muttered while typing in the search bar.

For hours, the only videos she could find were embarrassing outtakes.

"All I can find are students tripping up the stairs, someone streaking, mispronunciation of names that rhyme with sex organ, or the valedictorian stumbling on their words. How am I supposed to act? What if my breathing exercise doesn't work? Will I make someone an overnight sensation because I was the freak doing a 'floppy fish' on the floor?"

In a state of near panic, she got up from her desk and paced the room.

What am I supposed to do? Can I skip graduation? No—Val and Kyle would be heartbroken. I can't do that to them, it's not fair.

Warning of an attack rippled up her spine.

"That's just great! I'll get a million laughs while Tom becomes even more popular. Why does everyone like him, he is mean, and is constantly putting someone down."

She flopped on her bed and began focusing on her

Chapter Fourteen

breathing. When the warning passed, she slowly got up and decided to head downstairs for a snack.

Valerie was sitting at the table enjoying a tea when Sara walked into the kitchen. It did not take long for her to notice something was off.

She is biting her nails. That's not like her.

"Sara, please, come sit with me."

She hesitated before joining her aunt.

Great, Val knows something is wrong. I am an open book.

"Honey, you know you can tell me anything. What's wrong?" Valerie asked.

"I'm just feeling a bit overwhelmed with everything. She rolled her eyes and said, "And slightly nostalgic."

"Those are normal feelings."

"But I . . . ah . . . it's nothing towards you guys, it's just." Feeling more uncomfortable by the second, she blurted, "I just wish my mom was here."

Valerie reached over and cupped Sara's hand into hers.

"I deeply miss Lila too."

It was at this time that both reflected on the past.

"Look, honey, I know it was not an easy road, but you did it. You are about to graduate and nobody can take credit for that. It was all you."

"All thanks to you and Uncle Kyle."

She lightly squeezed her hand.

"You're wrong. We were blessed to have you live with us, but we didn't go to classes, study or take the tests. It

81

was you. And as for you coming to live with us, we would not have wanted it any other way."

Kyle walked into the kitchen and smiled at the sight of them holding hands.

Without saying a word, he filled three plates and brought them to the table.

"You girls know I love you, right?" he asked.

"We love you too," they replied in unison.

Neither made it apparent they did not notice him enter.

After dinner, Sara tried to help Val with the dishes but she would not allow it. She knew Sara was anxious and wanted her to rest.

The next morning, Sara woke extra early. She decided to prepare breakfast for both her aunt and uncle. She felt it was the least she could do, after all they had done for her. She made sure to prepare some of her mother's famous waffles, scrambled eggs, toast, bacon, sausage, and, well, let's just say it was one delicious spread. With the smell of bacon, and brewing aroma of coffee, it did not take long for the house to wake.

Sara was delighted to see Valerie and Kyle enter the kitchen.

"Please have a seat, guys."

"Wow, this looks amazing Sara."

"Thanks, Uncle Kyle."

"I agree, it smells great," said her Aunt.

Once they all gathered to enjoy their breakfast. It was time for Sara to prepare for graduation.

Chapter Fourteen

Excited for the day, Valerie bought Sara a beautiful dress. She wanted her to feel special and made sure the dress matched Sara's soft green eyes. It was a perfect match.

Sara searched her room for the cap and gown, but could not find it.

When she entered the kitchen to ask for help, Valerie was pressing it for a second time.

She broke into laughter and teased, "It's not an elephant, there is no way it grew wrinkles over night."

Kyle joined in.

"You know Val, she's excited, and whenever she gets excited she turns into a clean freak."

"What do you expect?" Val said while turning the iron off. "Our little girl became a woman overnight. "

A few hours later, it was time for Sara's big moment.

When the music started, the students began their march. Feelings overwhelmed with a mixture of sadness and pride, Valerie broke into tears. She turned and shoved the video camera into Kyle's hand.

"You said I shake too much to run this," Kyle teased.

"Not today," she admitted. "I'm so proud of her, and . . . and I keep thinking of Lil—." She stopped when Sara stepped into sight.

"Don't worry, I'm holding it steady," whispered Kyle. He was trying his best to hold in his emotions.

Val leaned in closer and admitted, "I know my sister. Death would not keep her from this—nothing could make her miss this day. She's here, I know she's watching, and she's proud."

Kyle took in a slow controlled breath and said, "You're right, honey. I'm sure Lila and your parents are here. They wouldn't miss this for the world."

Sara smiled when she saw tears in her uncle's eyes. As a child, she saw him as a superhero. Once the doctor's diagnosed her with stressed induced grand mal seizures and explained the symptoms, soon after, her uncle somehow knew when she was about to have an episode and would pull her out of them. She fought back a snicker when she heard him sing, "My uncle senses are tingling. Do you need ice-cream?"

I guess even superhero's have their moments, she thought.

For some odd reason those memories triggered images of her father.

No! Her mind screamed. *I refuse to give him my tears or a second thought!*

She took her place and began heading down the aisle as they called the name of each graduate. Everything came together when the principal called her name. She nervously marched on stage and accepted her diploma with pride.

Chapter Fifteen

After graduation, Sara quickly gained control of her life.

Therapy helped, it brought her to a good place. By the end of that summer, Sara was looking forward to her future. She set goals and enrolled into culinary school. She wanted to operate her own catering company.

Her acceptance letter arrived three days before she had to move. Sara did not panic. She packed her bags and embraced her new future.

Time flew. With less than a year to go, Sara would soon hold her certificate. The old Sara would have been terrified and suffered panic attacks, but not the new Sara. She was excited and ready to face her future.

One day, Valerie received a call from Grace Weston, an old high school friend who was the owner and Executive Chef of a well-established catering business. Grace was looking for a Sous Chef, and had heard about Sara's talent. That day, Sara was running late. Valerie took all the information down and tried to remain busy until her niece came home.

She arrived just in time for dinner.

Valerie could hardly contain herself.

The moment Sara sat down to eat, Valerie blurted, "I have some very exciting news for you!"

Sara's confusion showed.

"What is it?"

"Sorry," Valerie said. She waved her hand in the air in a motion much like someone wiping chalk off a board. "I'm just excited. Eat first, I'll tell you after dinner."

"Come on now, don't keep us in suspense," said Kyle.

"This afternoon, I was talking to my good friend Grace. She said she's looking for an assistant to help with her catering company."

Sara's eyes widened.

"An assistant—really? Assisting how?"

"Yes. Well, isn't that what a Sous Chef is? The second in command, right? I am sure those are the words she used, that she needed Sous Chef. Anyhow, guess who I recommended?"

Knowing she had not quite finished school, Sara replied with sadness, "I haven't a clue."

"You!"

Sara could not believe her ears.

"But what about school? I'm not ready—do you think I'm ready?"

"Yes. You're ready and she'll work with your schedule."

"I agree with Val," said Kyle.

Sara was ecstatic. She knew the job would not only give

her the experience she need, but with hard work, it could open the door to endless opportunities.

"You said you wanted to run your own company," said Valerie. "And if there is one person who will make it happen—it's Grace."

For a slight second, Sara began to feel nervous. There was a time when she would let her emotions control her, but not this time. With a jagged breath, she pushed her fear aside.

Valerie grabbed her hand.

"Are you alright? I didn't mean to upset you."

She slowly exhaled, while internally thanking the Dr. Baker for teaching her control.

"I sure am," she replied. "When do I get to meet her?"

"She said that if you were interested, she'd like to meet with you early as next week. She's leaving for a big job, but you can meet her at her Office in Raleigh."

"Did you say—I mean." She collected herself and tried again. "Does she live in Raleigh?"

"Yes, dear. That's where you'd be working."

Suddenly, Sara's mouth went dry. She took a short pause to sip her water. As she carefully placed the glass on the table, she said, "Sounds perfect."

"Don't worry, honey, we are only three hours away from you."

"I am ready for this," Sara said with a slow continuous nod. "I'll admit, I'm a bit nervous, but I'm ready." She looked up and smiled at her aunt and uncle. "It's time. I'm ready to venture out on my own."

For the remainder of the night, Sara focused on what she needed to do. She felt slightly overwhelmed. Instead of giving up, she turned to God.

"Lord, I really want this to work out. Please help me to stay strong."

Chapter Sixteen

One cold November day, Garrison headed to church. He sat in the pew behind mutual friends of Kyle and Valerie. It was his way of feeling a little closer to his daughter.

His felt as if his prayers had been answered when he overheard the couple in front of him talk about Sara.

"She's making a trip back for job opportunity, and from what I understand, there's a good possibility she will get the client. People say she might move this way," whispered the woman.

Like a stone statue, he sat perfectly still while his mind raced.

This could be my one and only chance!

Unfortunately, Garrison was the only one who seemed overjoyed.

The couple in front of him continued to talk.

For a moment, he tried to forget what ramifications his drinking had caused. Instead, he thought of chance meeting.

The anniversary of Lila's death is nearly upon us. Maybe Sara will show. She could see how I've been taking great care of Lila's site. Maybe a caretaker or someone who is visiting a nearby grave will tell her how often I visit, and how I am no longer the same—

"Val said," the woman's whisper interrupted his thoughts. "Whenever he calls he says he wants to know how Sara's doing. Why would they tell him? He has to prove he's changed."

"He has," replied her husband.

"No he hasn't."

"How can you say he hasn't changed?" snapped her husband. "Think back. He goes to church now, probably more than we do. That's the first sign of change. Plus he showers, he shaves, and besides . . . who are we to judge?"

She glanced over her shoulder and locked eyes with Garrison.

He forced a smile and gave a cordial nod.

Her face-pinked seconds before she spun back around. She sat erect with her head facing forward.

Valerie made it clear that I was to stay away, but I can't! It goes against my promise to Lila.

After mulling it over, he decided he would respect Sara's space. He did not want to harm her chance at obtaining a new contract.

Her career matters, besides, tomorrow is a big day. The doctor said my test results are in. I won't say or do anything until I know if the chemo has worked.

For the remainder of the sermon he kept fantasizing on

how great it would be to see and build a relationship with Sara.

I wonder if she still rides. She loved the horses. That kind of love doesn't fade. Is she happy with her career choice? I wonder if she chose that career so she could move this way. No, that can't be it. Valerie and Kyle love Sara. She's not a prisoner, she's happy. They gave her what I should have given her.

The next morning, Garrison made sure he was at the doctors early. The wait for his appointment seemed to last much longer normal.

When the Dr. Rogers entered the examination room, Garrison stood to shake his hand.

The doctor did not notice. He was looking down at the open file he was carrying.

"I'm afraid the results are not what we hoped for," said the doctor. He looked up from the file, saw Garrison's hand, and shook it. "Please, have a seat."

"Just tell me, Doc."

"It seems you are no longer in remission. We ran another set of scans, and, I am sorry, but it seems the cancer has come back. It is aggressive and has spread."

"What are you saying?"

"I am sorry, but it seems the chemo did not work." With a somber expression, he leaned forward and said, "Garrison, I have known you for years. I will not sugarcoat this. The truth is—your chance for survival is not good. I want to offer you hope. Scientists are constantly searching

Chapter Sixteen

for a cure. I have watched you change your life and you are not without options."

Feeling jaded, Garrison muttered, "Like what?"

"Some patients have been successful with alternative treatment."

"You mean holistic medicine?"

The doctor nodded.

"That is an option. Garrison, do not underestimate the power of the mind. However, I was suggesting you sign up for a clinical testing. I can set you up with a new trial, even if the medication does not work for you, the reports and testing will help better the product, which may very well save countless lives."

Garrison did not respond.

"If you like we can try a more aggressive chemo treatment, however, I do not think your heart or body will handle it."

The doctor continued to explain everything in detail.

"Because of the severity of your circumstance, I would like to give you a few minutes to consider the clinical testing. I'll tend to my next appoint and then we'll discuss your decision."

For twenty long minutes, Garrison mulled over everything. How the chemo made him feel. What the more aggressive route would do to his body, and the chance of him surviving the trial.

If I die during treatment, I could lose my chance to see Sara. I can't take that chance!

Chapter Sixteen

When the doctor returned, Garrison's mind was made. He blurted, "No, Doc, I am done with chemo!"

"Garrison, don't you want to try to extend your life?"

"What's the point? I could die before I fix everything!"

"Anything is possible," said Dr. Rogers while placing a hand on Garrison's shoulder. "Don't lose hope. If there is one thing I've seen too many times over the years, it's that when my patients lose hope, they soon lose their will to live. Fight, Garrison, fight back and let everyone see the man I see."

Feeling weak in the knees, Garrison dropped into the chair and admitted, "I'm sorry. You're right. I had a weak moment." He let out a heavy sigh as he buried his face in his hands.

"I'll give you a few more minutes."

"It's not needed, Doc. I'll do it. I have to try."

Chapter Seventeen

Within a few short months since Garrison's latest diagnosis, his condition spiraled downwards. The chemo was not working. His cancer was spreading faster than expected, and it got to the point where he too weak to function on his own.

The oncologist suggested hospice care and recommended he get his final affairs in order.

Like many, Garrison had difficulty accepting the idea of having strangers take care of him. The doctor explained it as a common element of the final stages, but he did not agree. He felt it was a punishment for what he had done.

"Lord, I wish I could have been able to see the error of my ways. Now I may never get a chance to make up with Sara."

Feeling exhausted, he closed his eyes and tried to think of happier times.

Much like watching a movie, he saw vivid memories of Lila writing while drinking her morning tea. A younger man walked into the room and kissed her on the top of her head.

At first, he felt enraged, but then he heard his own voice ask, "What are you writing?"

She looked up and smiled.

"My daily letters." She laughed lightly and teased, "Do you ever listen?"

"I do, but I don't understand why you do it."

"They are therapeutic." She flipped back a few pages and lightly ran her fingers over a large section. "Whenever the struggles seemed too difficult, I look back and read my previous battles. I don't know how or why, but, somehow, it gives me the strength to continue fighting."

His eyes shot open when something warm tickled the side of his face. "Enough of this wallowing," he said while bringing his hand to his cheek.

Feeling inspired by the short memory, he slowly got up and retrieved a pad and pen from the side table. In little time, the words were flowing. It was as if the pen was able to read his mind. He wrote everything from the day Sara left to the moment he picked up the pen. The letter included his regrets and his hopes for her future.

"Lila was right, that was therapeutic," he said as he folded the letter in half.

During the night, Garrison's mind wrestled with many of the regrets he had written down.

The one that influenced him the most was hiding his condition from Sara.

Chapter Seventeen

I'm a proud fool, he internally scolded. *I tried to convince myself that everything I did was for Sara. Telling her about the cancer is the best protection a father could give. The same disease struck both her parents. She has twice the risk of getting it. I'm a proud, stupid, fool!*

"Not anymore," he said aloud. "From my lips to God's ears, I will do the right thing."

The next morning, he woke early and waited until he was sure Valerie and Kyle were awake. When it was time to call, fear and pride nearly consumed him.

In a robotic fashion, he picked up the phone and forcefully pressed each button.

I will not give them a chance to hang up. No matter who answers, I will tell them everything.

For the first time since losing Sara, words he never considered raced through his mind, *Please don't let Sara answer the phone.*

Chapter Eighteen

After six consecutive rings, Garrison hung up. He sat down and watched the clock. Every fifteen minutes he tried again.

Two hours later, Valerie answered.

"Val. Don't hang up!" he practically demanded.

"Why do you keep calling? You know what I'm going to say and do."

"Please, this is important."

A loud and heavy sigh followed.

"One minute! That's all I'm asking for. I promise, after you hear me out, I'll never call you again."

"What is it now?"

"The reason I'm contacting you is because I have no way to reach Sara, and she needs to know—"

She interrupted him in midsentence, "We have discussed this!"

He fought to remain calm.

"Obvious you're still mad, but—"

"Can you blame me?"

Chapter Eighteen

"No," he said, "I don't blame you at all. I respect tenacity, but this is important. It's for her safety."

Much to her surprise, she believed him. She did not know how or why, but her told her to listen.

"Fine." She brought the phone closer to her mouth and whispered, "Tell me. And if I think it is important, I'll tell her."

Say it, before she changes her mind!

"I'm dying," he blurted.

Shocked by his response, she replayed his words in her head. A full minute crawled by.

His mind raced while he continued to stare at the second hand on his watch, *Is she still there? Did she hang up? No—I didn't hear a click. But what if she hung up at the same time I was talking? What if there's a storm and her phone line is down? Dear, God! I don't know what to do. Maybe she put the phone down and went to get Sara.*

After another thirty seconds, he asked, "Valerie, Valerie—are you still there?"

"Yeah . . . um, what did you say?"

"I'm dying. I was diagnosed with cancer."

"Garrison! How dare you," she shouted. "Is this some sick and twisted attempt to hurt Sara? Look, I meant what I said—I will never, EVER, let you hurt her again!"

"I am not making this up."

"Prove it," she challenged.

The second he began talking, she rushed to the computer desk. Each time he mentioned a doctor's name, she looked them up. Guilt crashed into her the moment she realized he was telling the truth.

"Stop," she said, "I know you're telling the truth."

"Thank you."

"Why didn't you tell us sooner?"

"I foolishly believed I could beat it, and to be honest, I didn't want to add more stress to your lives."

"I'm sorry but I can't tell Sara."

"You don't think this is important?"

"I do, but I also think she needs to hear it from you."

"Do you really think that's a good idea?"

"Yes. I believe it is. Don't get me wrong, I'll do it, but I truly believe you should. I'll give you a week, if you haven't told her by then, I'll do it. But understand, this is probably your only shot at possibly talking with her. She is still hurting."

"I understand. How is she? Is she alright? Do you want to give her my number or how do I contact her?"

"A few months ago, she landed a job with one of my friends. She's talented and is nearly ready to start her own catering business."

He smiled and took a long pause.

"Garrison," Valerie said with warning. "I'm sorry for what you are going through, but I meant what I said, I will never let you hurt her again."

"Thank you for protecting her."

Keep your guard up, Valerie's mind warned.

Chapter Eighteen

"Yes. Now, I'm going to give you her number. Don't over think this. Call her. You've made enough mistakes."

"Don't worry, I will."

Chapter Nineteen

Sara's eyes shot open to the sound of her answering machine.

"Hello—hello, Sara, Sara are you there? Dammit! I'm sorry but I am completely freaking out! I have some terrible news and I need help. I know you and Grace know a tonne of people and cater nearly everything. Grace assured me that you could handle everything including the planning, and I don't know who else to call. Can you hear me? Are you there? I'm going to assume you're checking the venue and that's why you haven't answered or returned my calls. I'm at my wits end. The seamstress contacted my maid of honor and—"

Two clicks ended the call.

"Why did she hang up? What did the seamstress say?"

A familiar robotic reminder chimed throughout the apartment, "Message box is full."

"Full?" she questioned.

In less than a year after relocating to Raleigh, Sara's life had shot into full gear with no sign of slowing down. She

Chapter Nineteen

quickly impressed Grace with her culinary skills. In the first month, Sara learned how to communicate with the clients. Soon, Grace was teaching her every role.

Sara loved every aspect of her job. Within eight weeks, Sara had grown not only as a caterer, but also as a confident team lead. She shared her hopes and dreams with her mentor.

Grace was intrigued when Sara opened up and shared her five-year plan. She explained how she would name the business after her mother, and how her catering company would provide full service. In her free time, Sara conducted interviews with young newlyweds. She noticed the brides all had the same complaint, too many contacts for one event. Sara's plan reduced the number of contacts the brides had to shuffle through, which helped reduced chances of miscommunication between the many different services.

Being a savvy business woman, Grace did not waste a moment. She provided Sara with a list of trustworthy florists, bakers, popular venues, and wedding planners. Grace's help provided Sara with all the tools she needed to launch her company. With Grace's name and Sara's tenacity, Lila's Catering quickly generated a profit for the two.

Didn't I check the machine when I got home?

The phone rang again.

In one swift motion, Sara whipped the blankets off, flung her legs over the side of her bed, and stood.

Chapter Nineteen

"Damn," she mumbled while shuffling her feet into a warm pair of slippers, "I forgot how cold it was last night." She rushed to the phone and snatched it off its cradle.

It was too late.

She pressed the last call button on the display to see how many times her worried bride had called.

"Seven times in less than two hours. I must have been in a deep sleep," she said while opening her note pad. She pressed play on her answering machine and began writing the bride's worries in point form.

Sara enjoyed every aspect of her job, including having to calm a panicking bride. By the fifth message, she already knew how to resolve the seamstress issue without affecting her important afternoon meeting.

If I can sign the Carter wedding, I'll have enough to payoff my loans. Lila's Catering will officially be mine.

A loud crack of thunder jolted her attention.

Dammit, it can't be. She opened her blinds and peered up at the sky. *There is no way I can show them my plans and the venue in this weather! They promised me two hours, and it took me three weeks to get that from them.*

In a near panic state, she turned on her laptop.

"Hi Sara," echoed her panicked bride, "I almost forgot to tell you that we changed our first dance song. Please call me back."

She quickly added the words 'new song' to her panic brides list before turning back to her laptop.

I'll call her after I see the afternoon forecast.

Chapter Nineteen

"Sara, it is nice to hear your voice. I'll try to call you back later today," said an unfamiliar man.

I'll have to check the display to see who he was. Not now! Nature, please be on my side, her mind begged as she scrolled to the hourly forecast. *This is not a good time for bad weather. The Carter wedding could make or break me.*

Nature was not on her side.

She noticed they were in for a long, cold and wet two weeks.

While controlling her breathing, Sara called her contact at the venue. After pulling a bunch of strings, she was able to take the Carters on a tour inside. She knew there was a private fashion show occurring in the ballroom. When she mentioned it was for the future Mrs. Carter, the event manager agreed to the tour.

"I guess it's true, money can move mountains," she said after pressing the end call button. She called her worried bride back and put her mind at ease.

That should just about do it. She thought while heading towards the washroom. *A hot shower and then a final check to make sure everything is ready before meeting the Carters. Oh wait!* She froze in place. *I better check the display. That could have been Mr. Carter who called. I better double check!*

"G. James," she exclaimed. "Why—how did he get my number?"

She tried to take in a controlled breath but could not do it.

No no no!

Chapter Nineteen

Her chest tightened, making it impossible to breathe.

This cannot be happening!

In a near panic state, Sara rushed into the kitchen and began opening and slamming each drawer, urgently searching for a paper bag. It had been nearly a year since she needed something to help control her panic attacks.

There were none.

"Dammit," she wheezed as she headed back to the living room.

She was desperate. She rushed to the closet to pull out her old laptop bag she used in college.

It has to be here, I don't have the time for this!

Feeling weak and helpless, she dropped to her knees and reached as far back as she could. The moment she felt the familiar fabric, she blindly unzipped and dug until she found her paper savior. She turned herself into a seated position with her back pressed against the interior wall of the closet, and brought the bag to her mouth.

Her eyes widened when she realized where she was.

"Damn you, Father," she said through clenched teeth.

It had been years since she sat in a closet, hiding from the monster and the shake attacks that terrified her. Her eyes scanned the closet for a focal point, while she desperately tried to take in a full breath.

It was too late.

Sara's body began to vibrate as the seizure took over. Her muscles contracted, and her head violently bounced against the wall. With each strike, she pictured the monster stomping through the house calling her name.

Her vision narrowed seconds before she lost consciousness.

Chapter Twenty

Garrison stared at the phone and pondered his next step.

Should I call her back?

He slowly stood and headed to the kitchen for a glass of water. While taking a sip, he replayed his message over in his mind.

My mouth was dry. Maybe my words sounded garbled. He leaned against the sink counter and replayed his message one more time. *Damn this cottonmouth! I cannot leave without calling her one more time. She needs to know.*

Time was no longer on his side. That afternoon he was heading into a hospice facility named, Spring Time Meadows.

Feeling weak and wanting to do the right thing, he headed back to the living room to redial Sara's number.

The phone rang at the exact moment he touched it. Without thinking he said, "Sara?"

"Hello, may I please speak with Mr. Garrison James?"

"That's me. Who's this?"

"My name is Abigale Brooks and I will be your fulltime attending nurse at S.T.M. Spring Time Mead—"

"I know what S.T.M. stands for," he interrupted.

"Yes," she said before clearing her throat. "Some patients experience forgetfulness and memory loss during their final step. We find it is best to explain who we are and what we'll be doing as clearly as possible." She paused when she heard him sigh heavily. "Mr. James are you alright, do you need an ambulance?"

"No."

"I need clarity. Are you saying you are not alright or that you don't need an ambulance?"

"I'm sorry, I'm fine. You can call me Garrison."

Another heavy sigh escaped him.

"Feel free to call me Abigale or Abby for short. At S.T.M. we strive to make those final steps as comfortable as possible. I'll be by your side until the end."

He knew they dealt with those who suffered from all addictions. His sponsor helped him research every facility in his state. The entire third floor staff at S.T.M. specialized in addiction rehabilitation. They knew what to say and do when recovering addicts had weak moments.

It had been years since Garrison fell of the wagon, and he swore he would not drink again.

He was relieved when Spring Time Meadows provided a contract swearing they would not buckle or allow him to drink, no matter how much he begged. He needed a facility that understood and would help him keep his sobriety promise.

"I know. That's why I was happy you had an opening before I died." He admitted, "I was making plans to die at home."

"It's understandable, and having said that, it is important that you know that I am also a friend who has been down the same path as you. I too was once addicted to alcohol."

"Really?" he asked with doubt.

"Yes. There is no reason for me to lie to you."

Of course she's telling me the truth.

"I'm sorry. It's been a hard couple of days," he admitted.

"You sound distressed, is there anything I can do to help?"

"I was trying to . . . well . . . maybe it's too late."

"Mr. James, I assure you, it is never too late."

Afraid he was about to make another terrible mistake with his daughter, he opened up and told the Abigale everything.

Not only did she understand, she promised to call Valerie and Sara while he was undergoing his tests and getting situated in his room.

Chapter Twenty-One

Heavy footsteps warned the monster was nearing.

"Where are you—you stupid girl?"

Knowing that if he found her the pain would be immeasurable, young Sara crawled out of her closet and carefully tiptoed downstairs.

As he entered the living room, she revealed herself.

"I am here, Daddy."

"Come here, NOW!"

She slowly walked towards him. Once within reached, her father grabbed her by the hair and dragged her through the house and into the kitchen.

"Look what you have done!"

"No, Daddy it was not me." She begged, "I didn't do it, I wouldn't."

"What are you saying? Are you blaming me?" he challenged.

"No, Daddy!"

He shoved her to the ground, and nearly rubbed her nose in the spilled beer.

"Clean it up or else."

Terrified, she crawled to the kitchen cupboard and pulled out an old rag. Before she could clean her body began to vibrate.

"What the hell is wrong with you?"

"Nnn . . . nnnoo . . . nn, nothing."

She watched as her father stepped over her and retrieved a new bottle of beer from the fridge. "It's a good thing your mother isn't here to witness this." When he stepped back over her, the bottom of his shoe scrapped across her nose. "This room better be sparkling clean when I came back or you'll wish you were never born."

As fast as her little arms would allow, she wiped up the floor, scrubbed the dishing and carefully tiptoed back upstairs to her closet. Shocked that she made it without feeling his strike, she crawled into the safety of her secret cubbyhole and curled herself into a tight ball.

A loud crash echoed throughout the house.

"You little—Sara, get in here NOW!"

Without thinking, she jumped to her feet and smashed her head against the wall. It caused a chain effect. He body vibrated as tried to crawl out, but it was too late.

Her vision narrowed as she lost control of her bladder and consciousness.

"Message box full," said a familiar robotic voice.

Sara slowly opened her eyes. She winced as a sharp pounding pain shot across the base of her skull.

Chapter Twenty-One

"It was a nightmare," she mumbled while trying to sit up.

The hard surface confused her. She carefully pressed her palms against the floor as she slowly sat up. Ice-cold liquid greeted her upper thigh and backside.

"What is that?"

The moment her hand touched the puddle she recalled everything that happened that morning.

Unbelievable! I haven't had an episode in so long. One phone call and I'm a complete mess—un-frigging-believable!

A bolt of lightening lit the entire apartment.

I don't have time for this.

After taking a few minutes to gather herself and make sure another episode did not follow, Sara slowly crawled out of the closet.

He did not call. I will not allow him or anyone to get in my way. I will be proud of myself and I will be successful despite my upbringing.

Once she had regained her strength, she cleaned the floor, had a quick shower and continued with her day.

Whenever her mind wondered to his message, she chanted, "I am Sara James, and I am no longer the product of Garrison James' abuse."

Chapter Twenty-two

After talking with Abigale on the phone, Garrison sat on the couch and fell into a deep trance. Andrea, his sponsor, had become not only an inspiration, but also his closest friend.

When his confirmation for Spring Meadows arrived, he contacted Andrea, who immediately drove over and helped him pack.

Andrea could not be there that day, he had to take care of personal business. Garrison understood. He sat on the couch with his prize possession in hand. It was the last family picture they took when Lila was alive.

Heavy knocking pulled Garrison out of his trance.

"Mr. James? We're here to take you now," said a soft female voice.

"Come in, I'm ready."

He debated on putting the picture into his suitcase, but decided against it.

"I don't have the energy to fight with that zipper."

Surprised by the sight of a large man entering his living room, Garrison looked up and tried to peer past him.

"Nurse Brooks is giving your neighbor the facility address where they'll forward your mail. My name is—."

"I don't care," barked Garrison.

"Not many do," replied the man with a light chuckle.

It made Garrison smile.

"I'm sorry, it's just hard."

"I understand, Mr. James. There is no need to apologize. Do you feel strong enough to walk or would you like to ride out in a wheel chair?"

"I'll walk," he replied as he slowly forced himself to stand.

"I'd be happy to take that picture and any bags you have packed, sir."

Garrison looked down at this hand and back to the driver.

"This is all I have left. I'll carry it."

"Sir? You don't have any bags? Are you aware that—"

"Yeah, yeah, my bag is right there," Garrison said while pointing to his suitcase. Realizing how rude he sounded. He stopped and looked up at the driver. "I was hoping I'd have everything done before leaving this house, it seems I've failed."

"It's fine." The kind driver placed a hand behind Garrison and helped him to the door.

Nurse Brooks rush through the door.

"I am so sorry, your neighbor was rather chatty." She

stopped and smiled at Garrison. "I'm Abigale. It's nice to put a face to the voice." Within seconds, she could see Garrison was stressed. She did not skip a beat. "Ronald, please take Garrison's bag, I need to go over a few things before we leave."

The driver slowly shook his head and replied, "Mr. James is a little upset."

"Yes," she said with a firm nod, "I'm aware of everything." She stepped to the side and motioned for the driver to leave. "We'll meet you at the car."

Nurse Abigale was good. She asked the right questions, and before leaving the house, she had both Sara and Valerie's phone numbers, as well as a letter addressed to Sara.

Once Garrison was situated in the back seat and confirmed he was comfortable, Abigale turned the radio onto his favorite station and softly mentioned he consider taking a nap.

He nodded as if he agreed, but he did not nap. Instead, he silently prayed.

Please forgive me, Lord. I know I was unkind and far from the father Sara or any child deserved. But, please, help me get this message to her. I ask she accepts the man I've become and will one day forgive me for my sins. I leave my life and heart in your hands and ask you protect her from those who wish harm.

He was so caught up in his thoughts the he did not hear the nurse calling out to him.

"What was that?" he asked.

Chapter Twenty-two

"We're here. Welcome to Spring Time Meadows. Now, you have some tests this afternoon and I believe I have some phone calls to make."

He let out a heavy sigh of relief.

It doesn't matter if she forgives or not. What matters is that Sara knows what to watch for. I don't want her dying the same way Lila did. Not only does it run on her mother's side but now with my current predicament Sara must really take good care of herself.

Chapter Twenty-Three

It was nearly midnight when Sara arrived home. After a successful meeting with the Carters, she received another emergency call from her worried bride and ended up spending the following seven hours assisting the bride.

"There is so much to do," she griped while taking six bags out of her trunk. "When did I say I'd make the guest favors? I thought the bridal party was making them?"

When Sara walked into the living room, the first thing she did was look at her answering machine. The bride, Francine had warned that she left a couple of messages earlier that afternoon.

Five messages! Frazzled Francine said she left a couple. Five is not a couple.

She setup the supplies on the living room floor and put the radio on low.

Over the following four hours, she created enough guest favors for three hundred and fifty guests, even though the bride assured her there would be no more than three hundred.

Sara knew better. Since taking on the account, the guest list continuously grows.

When she noticed how late it was, she opted to sleep on the couch. It was her way of preventing a deep sleep.

The next morning, Sara listened to the messages on her machine. Four out of the five messages were from her worried bride. She was relieved when she noted all concerns were completed.

The fifth message confused her. She wrote down the number and decided to get ready before returning that call. After a hot shower and good breakfast, she decided to return the call.

"Good morning, Spring Time Meadows, how may I help you?" said a soft female voice.

Nope, that's not the same voice.

"Good morning. My name is Sara James. A Ms. Abigale Brooks called my home. She left a message stating she needed to speak with me in regards to a patient in your facility."

"Would you happen to know the patient's name or room number?"

"No, the message on my machine was brief."

"That is good," said the operator. "We tend to leave little information on machines, in case we accidently dial the wrong number."

"I understand, privacy is important."

Sara could hear the woman type.

"Ah, here it is, I'll transfer you right away."

Chapter Twenty-Three

While Sara awaited the transfer, her mind raced.

What if it's about my father? For the first time in years, the man finally calls, and now someone from Spring Time Meadows calls. It sounds like a retirement facility. How do I react? What do I say if she mentions his name?

"Nurse Abigail Brooks speaking, how may I help you?"

"Yes, hi, I'm Sara James. You called my house yesterday?" she asked with hesitation.

"Thanks for calling back, Ms. James."

"You're welcome. Can you explain the reason for your call?"

"Yes. Ms. James. Your father's health has taken a turn for the worse. He is in our hospice facility, and his time is limited. The doctors feel he may have possibly a week."

"Um . . . alright."

"Yes," continued the nurse. "It is my understanding that your father attempted to contact you through you guardians. He was unsuccessful in all attempts excluding last week."

"I don't know anything about that," Sara admitted.

"I have his journal here and I assure you he has. Anyhow, yesterday, he was undergoing treatment. I offered to continue his calls. It is important that he speak with you, since you are his only living relative, and what he has to say involves your future."

Something sharp pressed against Sara's upper thigh. Her eyes widened when she looked down and saw her hand tremble rapidly, forcing the pen she held into her. She gasped and threw the pen clear across the room.

"Ms. James? Are you still there? Is everything alright? Hello?"

She did not register the nurse's call.

"Ms. James," Abigale repeated in a near shout.

"Yes, I am still here!" She let out a heavy sigh before coldly stating, "Look, I'm sure you think you're telling me the truth, but I'm no longer a naïve child. I have to look into a few things before I decide if I'll see him or not."

"Very well."

As Sara hung up the phone, she immediately let out a loud scream.

Chapter Twenty- Four

After taking a few moments to collect herself, Sara called her aunt.

Valerie was honest and admitted to Garrison's biannual calls. She also explained how her and Kyle never gave him a chance to explain his reason for each call.

"I feel terrible," said Valerie, "but in the beginning, he called when he was in a drunken rage. He felt we stole you from him and he often threatened to take you from us."

"So he hasn't changed."

"You're not listening," Valerie said with authority. "I said in the beginning. Honey—" She paused before continuing. "I have friends who go to the same church your father goes to. It's the same church you all went to as a family. About a year after you left, Garrison returned, and faithfully went every week. He did change."

"Why didn't you tell me?"

"Because of your nightmares, your panic attacks, you hiding in the barn and until . . . until you had things under control, we couldn't take the chance!" Valerie hiccupped in a couple of breaths before saying, "We didn't want to risk you reverting back into those horrible seizures. It tore our hearts out. When you had one, there was nothing we could do besides watch you struggle through it."

"When did you learn he was dying?"

"A few days ago, and I gave him your number right away."

After a long pause, Sara admitted, "I don't know what to do."

"Go to him. I think you need to hear him out, and don't you think it's time to make peace with the past?"

"I honestly don't know. What if he—I just don't know."

"Sweetie, you are a strong woman. You are no longer that frail, fearful little girl. Go, it's the right thing to do."

"Let's hope so."

"Do you want us to fly down to be with you?"

"No, Aunt Val, I think you're right. I have to do this on my own."

"If you change your mind for any reason, remember, we're only a phone call away."

"I will. I love you guys."

"We love you too, darling."

After hanging up, she immediately packed her suitcase. She knew if she took too long thinking things over, she might back out.

While on her computer searching for the quickest flight, she contacted her team and explained she had a family emergency. Sara could not walk away, not even for a day, without knowing everything would continue moving forward as if she was there. She contacted Carl, her other right hand.

"I am not sure how long I'll be gone. It could be a day or possibly a week. I will need you to handle all the preparations."

"You go and handle things, we will take care of everything at this end," he assured her. "Believe me, everything will be fine."

"I'm waiting for the Carters to decide. No matter what—"

"I'll call you," Carl interrupted. "I know the drill. We've got this. You go take care of things. If they call, I'll call you right away. They won't even know you're out of the city."

Sara decided to book her flight for the next red eye. She did not book a round trip, instead, she made sure she had a car rental agreement set on a day-by-day basis.

She spent the rest of that day and night delivering the guest favors to her worried bride. She reorganized her schedule and gave Carl a copy of her upcoming meetings.

Whenever she tried to get some rest, her mind would race. She tried to contact Dr. Baker but could not get through. She knew the doctor was away, but had hoped she checked her messages.

She made herself a promise.

If I feel myself losing it, I'll leave. Those are my terms. He can take it or not.

Feeling at her wits end, she headed to her laptop to

cancel her flight when the phone rang. It seemed Doctor Baker contacted her general practitioner and suggested antianxiety meds for the flight and visit with her father.

Chapter Twenty-Five

It was an eerie morning when Sara landed in Minneapolis. While putting her coat on, she walked sluggishly to the baggage claim. She was exhausted and slightly upset that she had taken the antianxiety medication.

It seems Aunt Valerie and Dr. Baker talk. I wonder how long this has been going on. What ever happened to patient and doctor confidentiality? Forget it—I'll deal with that when I get home.

While standing at the claim area, she read over her emails on her phone, and was surprised to learn that Dr. Baker already knew about her father's condition. It seemed Valerie was able to fill her in on everything. Frustrated and exhausted, she made a metal note to address the situation after she returned.

"I wish I would have thought of a coat. It looks like it might snow outside," said a woman talking with her travelling companion.

Sara looked over and saw the woman point her way.

"I warned you about the temperature," said her friend. "You never listen."

She turned away from the two and smiled.

So many times Father's alcohol took precedence over heat and electricity. I may not remember much, but there is no way I could forget those cold days and nights. With the upcoming weddings, I have to take preventative measure to avoid getting sick. I will not allow him to ruin my future.

Once she cleared customs and got the keys to her rental car, she headed to the parking garage. No sooner did she feel the cool air that her heart began racing.

I hope it's not another panic attack.

She focused on the car and slowly took in calming breaths. Once she made it to the car, she tossed her bags into the back seat and scurried into the driver's seat.

As she adjusted the rearview mirror, she saw something glisten on the side of her cheek. She quickly turned the mirror towards herself. "What is wrong with me?" she asked her reflection. "Nothing! I can do this. I am a confident business woman and he is my past."

But why do I feel ripped off?

She took in a deep breath and said, "Because everyone walked on eggs shells and didn't tell me the truth. I'm looking at things wrong. I'm here to find out the truth and that's all. Did he really call? I want to see that journal the nurse saw. Did he really change and what could he possibly say about my future, since he doesn't know me? He doesn't know anything about me or what I've been through. Sure, he may have talked with others, but unless it was me, he only heard half-truth. I'll be open minded and face the real Garrison James. Maybe my prayers were answered and the monster left. It's too bad it didn't leave when I was kid, but at least it's gone—if they are telling the truth."

She wiped her tears away and gave a hard nod at her reflection.

"That's what I'll do. I'm going to face him, I'll demand I see his journal, and I'll see for myself if what he has to say really matters."

The moment she turned the key over, the dashboard lit up and she noticed the time.

Dammit, I wonder what time visiting hour is.

She dialed Spring Time Meadows and was disappointed to learn she had three hours before she could face Garrison.

"Screw it," she said as she put the car in drive. "I'm not going to sit here. I'll stop by the old house. He's not there, and I'm sure the new owners will be friendly. If not, maybe I'll go to the ranch and see if I can feed the horses."

The second she turned onto the main street, the roads seemed familiar. To Sara, it felt as if she was in auto drive. *It's been years and yet, nothings changed.* There was a strange feeling in air.

She turned into the driveway. The moment her eyes focused on the abandoned house, her mind quickly filled with horrid flashbacks of the raging monster stalking the grounds for her.

She fought to push them out.

"Can I really face him?" she mumbled while looking past the house to the large barn. "He used drink in there while Momma suffered."

The stables were not far from the barn. She overheard her aunt talk about how Garrison had lost or was about to lose everything. Her eyes shifted between the house and barn.

"Forget it! The house looks abandoned. I'll checkout the barn and stables. Maybe the new owners are working on the farm and living somewhere else. God know the house would need major renovations. I'm sure the stench of stale alcohol and vomit will not be easily removed. They'll probably have to replace the walls and floors."

She turned to car onto the gravel drive that led to the barn and slowly drove. She noticed a few horses trotting towards the stable behind the barn.

Someone must be tending the stable. I'll tell them who I am and ask if it's aright to walk around.

Memories of pitiful glares and unsympathetic whispers teachers and parents made whenever she asked for help flashed through her mind. She stretched her neck towards the rearview mirror until her eyes met their reflection and said, "Don't be stupid. If you tell them who you are, they'll tell you to leave."

Rage boiled in the pit of her stomach.

Chapter Twenty-Five

"Nobody tried to help. Nobody listened. They turned a blind eye and felt pity for him. They saw the bruises." She flopped back in her seat. "The teacher asked if I was being bullied. I told her the truth and asked for help, and that's when she said to give him time, he's hurting, and be a good little girl." Her jaw tightened as her rage grew. Through clenched teeth, she said, "All they did was feel sorry from my father. What about me? What about the little girl who had to live with him? God! When I think of the number of times I heard them say 'the poor man, he is heartbroken', it makes me sick."

Feeling anger towards others surprised Sara.

I thought I was angry at him for letting the monster take over. It seems I'm angry with everyone. She thought it over and wondered, *Why didn't Dr. Baker see it or help me see it?*

She pulled the ignition key out and mumbled, "It's my own fault. The only person I wanted to talk about was my mother. Aunt Valerie and Uncle Kyle walked on eggshells around me. They thought talking about my mother would upset me. They didn't understand that her memory was fading. I was afraid I'd lose her if I didn't talk about her."

After dabbing her tears away, she stepped out of the car and headed towards the barn.

"Miss. Excuse me Miss," shouted a man.

Wrapped up in her own thoughts, she did not hear him.

"Miss," he shouted.

She stopped.

"Over here Miss."

She turned and saw a man who looked to be around the same age as her approach. He smiled and said, "I am sorry if I startled you."

"It's fine," she replied.

"I'm Mitch Anderson."

The moment she heard his name she recognized him.

"Miss, is there something I can help you with?"

"Wow, it's been years."

"It has?" he asked.

"Mitch it's me, Sara James."

"No way!" he said with a bright smile. "Sara, how are you?"

Mitch was one of Sara's only friends. They sat together at Sunday school. When her family stopped attending church, they continued their friendship and shared every recess together.

"Wow," he said. "It's been a long time. I'd hug you but I've been working in the stables. How are you?"

"I'm alright." She looked around and admitted, "So much has changed. Did your family buy the farm or did you?"

He took a moment to study her. He knew the reformed Garrison James and not the monster Sara knew.

"I work for you dad," he replied with confusion. "It's how I'm paying my way through college. I love it here and thanks to your dad, I already have hands on experience."

"As what?"

"A veterinarian, I'm in my final year. If it wasn't for your dad—I don't know if I could afford school."

Sara did not know what to say.

"I'm sorry about your mom and everything. You left without saying goodbye."

"It was sudden, and the right thing to do," she admitted.

An awkward silence surrounded them.

"Why are you here?" Realizing how his question sounded he quickly reworded it. "I mean, are you here to visit your dad?" He chuckled and lightly shook his head. "Wow, can you tell I'm nervous?"

"You're nervous?" She asked, "Why are you nervous?"

"Because of you. What I meant was . . . are you aware that you father is in hospice? I'm taking care of things here, but he couldn't wait any longer, he had go. Things aren't . . . Sara, it doesn't look good."

"I know. That's why I'm here."

Mitch let out a sigh of relief.

Wow, he's concerned for him.

"I thought I'd visit the farm before visiting him."

"Oh, well, it took a lot of work but the place has come around. We have two fillies and ten boarders. That's not including mine or your father's horses." He began walking towards the barn. "Come on, I'll show you."

"Boarders?" she asked. "When did he reopen the stable?"

"The day he got his one-year chip for sobriety."

He knows the truth.

"How long ago was that?" she asked.

"Like I said, everything's changed. I've been working on the farm since I was a kid." The moment their eyes met, he smiled and admitted, "Your dad's not just my boss, he's a friend. He earned his one-year chip two or three years after you moved. He's been sober ever since."

"That's nice."

That's nice? Did I really say that?

He headed into the barn.

"Follow me."

While following him inside, she looked around and was amazed with all the improvements they made. She could see the hard work Mitch put into the building. She noticed he patched up the hole in the roof and replaced the broken and missing stable doors.

"Amazing," she mumbled.

"It was a lot of work, but your dad and I did it."

Mitch opened up and told Sara everything him and her dad had worked on over the years. He explained how hard it was to watched Garrison battle his illness. That he liked her father's sponsor, and how he looked up to Garrison and admired his strength.

Sara's anger towards her father began to fade. It confused her.

I've got to get out of here. I can't continue to let others affect my judgment.

"It's been great catching up, but I've got to go."

Mitch rushed over to the sink and washed his hands.

Chapter Twenty-Five

"Do you really have to go?"

"I am afraid so."

He dried his hands and looked at his watch.

"Wow, time flies. Visiting hours start in thirty minutes."

"Yeah, and I'm only here for a few days."

Mitch stepped in closer and asked, "Only a few days?"

She nodded.

"I have to get back home, business is picking up."

"I heard."

"You heard, from who?" she asked.

"From your father," he said with a light chuckle. "He said you're a successful caterer."

It surprised her. Her mind raced, but no matter how hard she tried, all her memories included a monster bellowing orders.

"So what do you think?" asked Mitch.

"What do I think? I think my aunt told him about my career."

He laughed.

"You're wrong."

"I am?"

"Yeah, don't you remember how the hens at church talk?"

"Not really," she admitted.

"Apparently you catered an event, and from what your dad heard, it was the best food they ever had. You were the talk of the church. Everyone was wondering if you'd bring your business here."

Chapter Twenty-Five

"Oh, I didn't know."

"So what do you think about joining me for dinner?"

Sara could feel herself blush.

"I don't know."

"You've got to eat," he said while reaching over the sink and taking a business card out of a small box. "Here's my card. Call me." The moment she took the card, he pulled her into a hug. "Call me, Sara," he whispered. "It's been too long."

Chapter Twenty-Six

As she got closer to her destination, she began to feel a cornucopia of emotions. She was anxious to see if her father really had quit drinking and changed. She felt anger at everyone, her aunt and uncle for not telling her he called. At Dr. Baker, because she recently learned that Baker talked with Valerie and her general practitioner, and did not mention anything to Sara. She also felt confused. When Mitch hugged her, she liked it and that bothered her.

Sara had dated before. She had her share of short-term relationships, and there was a time when she thought she was in love, but never had a hug felt so right.

When she pulled into the parking lot, she fought hard to press her feeling aside.

Treat it like a business meeting. You cannot provide a dream event until you have all the facts. The same goes here. I will not address the monster or Garrison until I know all the facts. Nurse Brooks said she had his journal. I want to read it before I see him.

Once she had control of her emotions, she forcefully

slammed her car door and stormed through the front doors.

"Good morning, how may I help you?" said the woman in the front office.

Sara hesitated before replying, "Yes. I would like to speak with nurse Brooks."

"Do you have an appointment?"

"No. Nurse Brooks is taking care of Garrison James. He is a relative of mine, she should recognize my name."

"Oh yes, Ms. James. Nurse Brooks was hoping you'd arrive," she said while bringing the phone to her ear and dialed. Sara tried to gain her attention but it was too late. "Good morning. Ms. Sara James is here to see her father."

Sara interjected, "I would like to see nurse Brooks first." Feeling slightly embarrassed, she looked to the floor, bit her bottom lip and began to sway from side to side.

"I will tell her right away." After hanging up, she stood and said, "Please follow me. I'll take you to the waiting area."

"Thank you."

Spring Time Meadows was a very large facility. It consisted of five floors. Before leaving, Sara researched as much as she could. She learned that it was one of the most prestigious hospices in all of Minnesota. Unfortunately, the entire place had the overpowering odor of antiseptics, and for a brief moment, it triggered her into a sneezing frenzy.

Once Sara finally stopped, the receptionist held out a tissue and said, "Bless you."

"Thanks," Sara sheepishly replied. She felt light headed and stopped in front of the elevators.

"Are you alright?"

"Yes," Sara said with slight nod. She noticed chairs lined along the wall across from the elevator. She asked, "Is she coming from a different floor?"

"Yes."

"Does the staff wear nametags?"

The receptionist slowly nodded.

She sat down and said, "I'll wait here."

The receptionist eyed her before finally giving in.

"Alright, Ms. James. I'm Rose and if you need me I'll be at my desk."

"Thanks," Sara said in a near whisper.

Once the receptionist was out of sight, Sara closed her eyes and concentrated on her breathing.

I can do this. Stay strong. I'll simply ask to see his journal. I won't explain why unless she denies my request. Then she'll learn about the Garrison James I knew.

A soft bell caught her attention. She opened her eyes and saw a robust woman step off the elevator. She wore a colorful uniform.

Not what I expected, she thought while searching for a nametag.

"Are you Ms. James?"

Chapter Twenty-Six

"Nurse Brooks," she stammered, "I mean, yes—yes I am."

The nurse pressed her hand against the elevator door. "Shall we head upstairs?"

"No. I don't think, I mean . . . I am not willing to talk with him until I read that journal you mentioned on the phone."

Nurse Brooks smiled.

"I understand. Ms. James, there is a quiet room on each floor. I'll escort you to that room and bring you your father's journals. Are you comfortable with that?"

Sara nodded. She was surprised with how easily the nurse accepted her condition.

Nurse Brooks moved to the side and motioned with her free hand for Sara to join her in the elevator. Once inside, the nurse took control. "Mr. James is on the third floor. The entire floor is dedicated to final step patients who are recovering from substance abuse. Many, like Mr. James, need special support. There is also a chapel on every floor, as well as support services for survivors."

"What do you mean by 'special support'?" asked Sara.

"All patients on the third floor fear relapsing. Some, like your father, sign an agreement ensuring we will not allow them to drink or contact someone to bring them personal supplies or substances. We check all bags and question visitors. It is not intended to offend, it is procedure."

"So you know the truth about him?"

Nurse Brooks nodded and said, "Yes, and once you read

his journals, you'll understand just how much I really know."

Sara's heart raced.

This is so confusing. I don't know if I can face him or not. I'm here for answers and to read his journal. Maybe I should call Aunt Valerie? NO! I can't rely on others. Look at the facts! They thought they were protecting me, but if he changed the way Mitch described, then they made a big mistake. I never wanted to leave my father. I wanted the monster to leave us.

"Are you alright, Ms. James?"

Her neck snapped up when she heard her name. The nurse was standing in the hall holding the elevator door open.

"I'm sorry, I didn't hear you?"

"I could tell you were deep in thought. I said your father is in room 362, it's the third door on the right side of the elevator. The quiet is to the left. It's the last room at the end of the hall. If you would like, I will retrieve the journals and meet you in the quiet room."

Feeling relieved, Sara whispered, "That's perfect." She waited for the nurse to say something else or head to her father's room. After an uncomfortable moment, Sara shifted her weight to the side and asked, "Is there anything else I need to know?"

Nurse Brooks gave a sympathetic smile and replied, "I'm holding the elevator door for you."

"Oh!" She rushed out of the elevator and headed towards the quiet room.

Chapter Twenty-Six

How embarrassing.

Chapter Twenty- Seven

Nurse Abigale hastily entered Garrison's room. He had a difficult night and she knew time was precious.

Garrison was asleep.

Should I wake him? she wondered. *No, he hardly slept. I know he would do anything to prove he changed.*

As quietly as possible, she carefully opened the side table drawer and retrieved his journals.

When she stepped out of the room, she noticed Sara was standing in the hall directly across from the quiet room.

She hurried to her side.

"Is everything alright," she asked.

Sara spun around to face Abigale. Her wide eyes warrant her shock.

"I'm sorry I startled you."

"It's fine," Sara replied.

"Why are you waiting in the hall? Is the room occupied?"

"I don't know," whispered Sara while pointing to the

sign posted below the room name. A small, mobile section easily slid between the words occupied and vacant. It hovered in the middle. "The door's closed and to be honest—I'm not sure if someone didn't slide it all the way to occupied or not. It's so quiet here, I'm afraid to knock, I might wake a patient."

"That's completely understandable."

After three light taps on the door, Nurse Abigale felt it was safe to proceed. She entered the room and waited for Sara to follow. She could tell Sara was anxious. Garrison opened up and told her everything. Worried that Sara might have an episode, she opened the blinds before leaving.

Like clockwork, every hour nurse Brooks checked Garrison's vitals. Once she was done, she headed down the hall and looked in on Sara. She never opened the door. She simply glanced into the window to see if she was alright. In the short time she had known Garrison, she felt for him. She feared Sara having a severe episode and being admitted into the hospital.

That evening, at five minutes after eight, Abigale looked into the quiet room. Sara looked up from the journal and glared into her eyes. Before the nurse had a chance to move towards the door, Sara slammed the journal onto the table and stormed out of the room.

"Does someone need the room or are you rushing me?" she nearly shouted.

"I'm sorry?" Abigale questioned.

Chapter Twenty- Seven

Sara let out a heavy huff.

"You're making me feel rushed! It seems like every few minutes you're looking through the window." Feeling slightly guilty, Sara placed her hand on the nurse's arm and said, "I'm sorry—I'm not trying to be rude. I know you've read his journals and you know what's happened, but I haven't read them. I needed those. Nobody said a word about his transformation!" She fought her tears while backing into the room.

Nurse Brooks did not skip a beat. She hurried in and closed the door behind her.

Sara picked up a journal and leafed through the pages.

"I have unanswered questions and I don't know if I can ask him."

"Ask me," replied Abigale, "I placed myself in your shoes and asked your father everything I could."

"Why . . . why would you do that?"

"Because I've been in your father's shoes. I was an addict," Abigale admitted. "I lost a lot and know how addictions can rip families apart." She sat on the couch and patted the seat next to her. "Ask me anything, and if I don't know the answer, I'll ask your father and relay it back to you."

Surprised by nurse Brooks kindness, Sara slowly sat down and asked with amazement, "You'd do that?"

"Yes, but I cannot give you his response until tomorrow."

"Why?"

"Because visiting hours are over. I understand that it felt as if I was checking on you every few minutes, but wasn't. Every hour I checked your father's vitals and then I checked in on you. Have you read both journals?"

"Yes."

"Good. That means you know your father knew you suffered from episodes. He did not recognize them, but I do and I explained them to him. I wanted to make sure you were safe."

"Thanks," Sara sheepishly said.

Nurse Abigale took the lead.

"So you have questions. Ask away."

Feeling stumped and slightly rushed, Sara could only think of one and wasn't sure how to word it.

Abigale noticed.

"Ms. James, what we say here is between us. I will not lie to your father, however, I will word things correctly. Say what you think. I'm sure there is a softer way to repeat it, if it needs repeating. I may have the answer. You're father and I have a mutual respect. It was earned by honesty and understanding, but lets face it. He is ill, and when people suffer through illness, they can be moody. I'm tough and I've been in his position. He knows my history and I know his."

Sara thought it over before giving a nod of approval.

"I've read every word, twice. I have a hard time believing these are his journals."

"Why is that?"

Chapter Twenty-Seven

"Well," said Sara while shifting in her seat. "The ink is the same, there is no date and the pages hardly aged. If he was making daily entries one book would be faded more than the other."

"You're right. Your father started writing in his journal towards the end. He said he dreamt of his Lila writing each day. Apparently it was something she used to do."

Sara nodded, even though she could not recall seeing her mother write. She was not sure if it was because of how young she was or if her mother wrote when she was alone.

Abigale continued, "He said your mother explained how writing everything down helped her remember the better times during her more difficult days. That was when he began writing, and, since he was an alcoholic, he could not recall all the dates. He wrote what he remembered from the day you left to yesterday—the day he arrived here."

Sara's mind began to race.

I was hoping he lied but I don't think he did. He wrote everything him and Aunt Valerie said to each other. Even things I didn't hear because I was upstairs. He even remembered the dress I wore that day.

Sara whispered, "Why was I hoping he lied in his journals?"

"For many of us, it's easier to dismiss the past than accept it, face it, and move on."

Surprised to hear an answer, Sara looked up.

"Sorry, I was wondering aloud."

"I know," said Abigale with a kind smile. "I was sharing my experience."

"I don't understand," Sara admitted.

"I had difficulty accepting what I'd done, facing those I'd hurt when I was an alcoholic, and moving on. I lost a lot and drinking helped me forget, but once I faced it, much like your father did, I was able to move on, continue life on a better path."

Sara understood, she took in a deep breath and said, "Is he awake? I'd like to see him now."

Nurse Brooks eyes saddened as she said, "I'm sorry, you'll have to come back tomorrow. Visiting hours have ended."

"Can I sit in his room?"

"We weren't sure you would show. I did not add you to the list and it is government policy. I will add you tonight and you can as of tomorrow." Abigale thought for a moment. "Do you have somewhere to stay? I can give you your father's house keys."

No! I can't go there yet. I have to talk with him and make sure everything he wrote is true. I remember my father and the monster. I'll know if it's really gone.

"No. I'll be fine," she said while standing and hooking her purse over her shoulder.

"Are you sure?"

Sara nodded and headed out the door.

Nurse Abigale understood. She waited until she heard

the elevator door open and close before retrieving the journals and returning to Garrison's side.

Once inside the car, Sara tried to find a hotel room. After several phone calls and learning there was a convention in town, she gave up.

Father's journal mentioned two of his friends Andrea and Thomas. Thomas was his sponsor and Andrea was also part of his AA and was there for him when Thomas was not around. He also mentioned Mitch. I have no idea who they are or how to contact them, but I do have Mitch's number. She thought it over.

That's what I'll do. I'll see if he's up for some company. Once I get some answers, I'll head back here. I can always sleep in the car, it's only one night.

Chapter Twenty-Eight

Sara woke to the sound of roosters crowing. She slowly stretched and paused the moment her hand touched a cool object. Confused by what she felt, her mind began to race.

What is that? Did I buy a new lamp? No, wait! I'm not home. Mitch insisted I stay at his house. I don't remember going to bed. She felt her body shift as she felt the familiar movement of someone rolling over. *No! Did I . . . or did we?*

In one quick motion, she sat up, looked down at what she was wearing, and then scanned the room.

Thank heaven!

Mitch was asleep on the opposite side of the sectional couch.

I know I felt attracted to him and the thought crossed my mind, but that's because he's so easy to talk with. I would never throw myself at another, especially not now. It's wrong and . . . it's just wrong.

When she called him, he invited her to come over for a visit. He ordered pizza and they talked until the early hours about everything. She was surprised with how easy it was to talk with him. She learned more about her father through Mitch than she could have hoped. By early morning, they had told each other everything. Their past relationships, her medical issues, and she even opened up and told him about the day she heard her father's message.

Mitch was warm and understanding. He opened up and admitted to the abuse he endured with an ex-girlfriend. She knew it happened but also knew that it was something not many men would talk about.

He looks peaceful. I'll write him a note and makes sure to visit before I return home.

She slowly tiptoed into the kitchen and wrote a note thanking him for the visit. As quietly as she could, she slipped out the front door and headed to the hospital.

Chapter Twenty- Nine

Sara took her time driving to the Spring Time Meadows. The roads were congested, but it did not bother her. Each time she checked her rearview mirror, she noticed her eyes were smiling.

It confused her.

Why am I happy? I'm about to face the man who at one time made my life a living hell. Is it because he's changed? How do I know for sure? She thought it over and continued her internal argument. *Nurse Brooks, the journals and Mitch all know him. They tell the same story. Think, Sara! Mitch had no idea he had a journal, let alone two. Aunt Valerie and Uncle Kyle made a mistake. They thought they were protecting me. It's not their fault, the didn't ask questions, and he said in his journal he always started the conversation the wrong way.*

The moment Sara walked through the front doors the receptionist stood and greeted her.

"Good morning, Ms. James."

"Good morning. Is it alright to head upstairs?"

"Actually, I need a moment of your time."

Chapter Twenty- Nine

"Why?"

"Nurse Brooks added you to our visitor clearance list. I need you to go over the agreement with you as well as give you your pass and badge."

Sara joined her at the front desk. While she completed the questionnaire and security agreement, a security officer approached her.

"Ma'am, will you please open your bag?" he asked, although it sounded more like a demand.

She slowly opened her bag.

"What's this all about? Why didn't anyone check my bag yesterday?"

"Mr. James is under twenty-four hour watch, however, Nurse Brooks informed us that you would have alone time. It is our fiduciary responsibility to check all bags to ensure substances are not brought to patients."

As if I'd bring him a bottle! Sara thought while yanking her purse open.

The security guard noticed her discomfort.

"Ma'am— it is nothing personal. It is the patient's final request. Everyone on the third floor voluntarily request assistance in assuring they continue their sobriety until the final day."

Guilt instantly set in.

Don't be neurotic, Sara! He's doing his job. Jeez, they're helping the patient's keep their sobriety, and here I am being difficult. Maybe I'm not ready for this.

The security guard quickly cleared her. While waiting

for the elevator she debated taking the stairs, but could feel eyes on her and decided against it. When the doors opened, she scooted in and darted an angry glare at the receptionist and security guard.

Nobody was watching her.

Damn—I really am neurotic.

When Sara arrived on the third floor and stepped off the elevator, she cringed at the sound of her heel clicking against the floor.

How could I forget? She wondered while taking her shoes off. *If I was smart, I'd have stopped to buy a pair of sneakers or slippers. Tomorrow, I'll pick up a pair after visiting hours so I don't make the same mistake again.*

When she made her way to Garrison's room, Nurse Brooks was checking his vitals.

"He's resting," Abigale whispered.

"Oh, should I come back?" mouthed Sara.

"No. It is a morphine induced nap." Nurse Brooks wrote in Garrison's chart. "You can whisper without waking him."

"I thought this floor was against substances. Morphine is a narcotic. Don't you worry about the patients relapsing?"

"No. Their medication is for pain management only and we monitor it closely. The doctor and one nurse must be in the room when distributing the medication." She looked down at Garrison and then back to Sara. "He can be a stubborn bird when he wants. He refused medication until his body and the doctor demanded it."

Sara sat in the seat next to Garrison's bed and admitted, "I don't understand."

"His vitals were high. Each time I asked him to rate his pain on a scale of one to ten, he said it was zero. I knew he was lying and called him on it. He told me 'it wasn't my business' and to do my job." Nurse Brooks chuckled before continuing, "I explained that bothering grumps like him was my job."

"Did it work?" Sara asked with a slight smile. She was learning so much and appreciated it.

"Not at first. It was a difficult night. He had little sleep and . . . he was worried."

"About what?"

A somber expression crossed Nurse Brooks face as she said, "You."

"Me? You didn't tell him I was here did you?"

"No."

"Thanks, I appreciate that."

"I didn't do it for you."

"What?"

Is she trying to fight with me?

"You remember "the monster". I believe that's what your father quoted you calling his drunken persona."

"Yes, but—"

"There is no but," interrupted Nurse Brooks, "I'm sorry if I seem too direct or harsh, but I am giving you the same respect I give your father. We will not lie or deny each other our true thoughts or feelings. He is about to die and he deserves to hear the truth."

Does she hate me?

Nurse Brooks walked across the room to her small workstation. She gripped the back of the chair with her left hand. She wheeled it to the space directly across from Sara and sat down.

"You're upset. That was not my intension."

You could have fooled me.

Nurse Brooks explained, "You demanded to read your father's journals before seeing him in person, correct?"

"Yes."

"Ms. James, I am not from around here, and what I know about you I read in those very same journals. Do you understand?"

"I'm not sure it's the same," Sara challenged.

"You're right. They are not the same."

Sara crossed her arms and glared into Abigale's eyes.

"How about you enlighten me and explain how they are not the same. You seem smug to me."

"Very well," replied Abigale. "Up until a short while ago, what you knew about your father was based off childhood memories. Correct?"

"Yes, we've established that."

"Please understand that I don't know you at all. I have no recollection of you whatsoever. The pictures Garrison showed me were that of a small child. From my point of view, you were a strange woman who declared she was his child and without proper identification, I had to take your word for it."

"So why'd you let me in?"

"Because of the journals. Garrison admitted his journals were a recent project he shared with no one. I was the first he told, he said he was afraid they'd think less of him or that they'd worry the cancer had spread to his brain. If you hadn't mentioned his journals I probably wouldn't allow you much time upstairs, and I'd never leave you alone."

"Do you want to see my driver's license?"

"No, it's not needed. Last night, I looked at the security footage and Rose confirmed your background check."

Feeling slightly insulted, Sara muttered, "Wow. Don't hold back on my account."

"I won't, and I hope you'll give me the same respect."

"This doesn't feel like respect."

"Maybe not." Abagail leaned forwards to ensure they maintained eye contact. "But as I was about to say, Garrison is not the only patient on this floor. Our job is to protect everyone, and believe me—dealers and addicts can be creative. I had no idea what you would look like or if you were coming. Then, suddenly, Garrison's daughter was here. You could have been a runner pretending to be Sara, and when I wasn't looking, you could have slipped the substance to someone in the washroom or at the elevator. That is why I couldn't allow you to stay here overnight. Not until we knew for sure you were the real Sara James."

"If you were so concerned then why did you let me stay in the quiet room by myself?"

"Didn't you meet Frank our security guard?"

Sara nodded.

"He monitors the stairwell and every floor. I would have known if you ventured out."

"Has anything like that ever happened before?"

"Yes, and it helps that everyone on this floor, excluding the doctors, have at one time been an addict. We shared our experiences with security, including our lows, and believe me—nearly everyone hits rock bottom before looking up."

Nurse Brooks is a straight shooter. I rather respect that and her.

"It's a deal," said Sara while stretching out her hand. "I appreciate your honesty and will give the same respect in return."

Nurse Brooks head spun towards Garrison seconds before his heart monitor beeped faster. She instantly stood, wheeled the chair to her desk and retrieved his chart.

"Is everything alright?" asked Sara.

"One moment please."

Dear God, he can't die, please, not yet!

The seconds slowly ticked by.

When Abigale finished her entry, Sara asked, "What should I do? Is there something I should do? Is he alright?"

"It appears he is dreaming."

"How can you tell?"

"His heart rate increased when he whispered the name Lila."

"I didn't hear him say that."

"You were talking."

"Are you sure?"

She looked up from the chart and saw fear in Sara's eyes.

"I am confident," she replied while tapping the monitor with the tip of her pen. "If you look here, you'll see his breathing is normal, almost calm for someone in his condition. His vitals are here, and they are fine." She pointed to her chart. "Here is the record of his vitals since his arrival, and as you can see they are maintaining. If a sudden spike or drop in his vital or breathing were to occur, the alarm on this machine would go off. I am not a doctor, my opinion is based off experience and training, but, if you would like a second opinion, I would be happy to get the doctor." She placed her hand on Sara's shoulder. "You hardly know me, and I can see that you're ready to meet your father. I assure you, I will do everything I can to help you meet him."

"You're confident it was dream?"

"I am confident his heart rate increased when he said the name 'Lila'."

That was a great answer. She should consider politics.

"Would you like me to get the doctor?"

"No. But could you direct me to the cafeteria? I'd like a drink."

"Your father should wake soon. I'll get you something from the kitchen, we have nearly everything, you name it and I'll get it."

"Shouldn't you be here when he wakes?"

"No. I promise, his heart is fine, and he'll be fine. Now—what would you like to drink?"

"Water I guess."

"There is a small book shelf behind my desk. Why don't you take a look, there could be something that interests you."

Nurse Brooks left before Sara had a chance to think up an excuse for her to stay.

Dammit!

Nurse Brooks returned with a small tray filled with food and drinks. Over the following three hours, they talked and got to know each other. They were on a first name basis and both liked each other's company.

As time moved on, Garrison began to stir. Without skipping a beat, Abigale got up and moved her chair into the hall.

"What are you doing?" asked Sara.

"We agreed that you and Garrison should talk. Now's the perfect time."

"But what if I'm not ready?"

Abigale smiled and said, "Sara, you flew here to see him. That's a clear sign you're ready."

"But what do I say?"

"It's up to you, but remember, be honest. You owe that to yourself." She winked and added, "And to him."

Chapter Thirty

"Where did my nurse go and who are you?" demanded Garrison.

Sara took in a deep breath in through her nose while she slowly turned to face her father.

Is it really him? It kind of looks like him, but, much older than he should and frail! He's lost so much weight. How can I say what needs to be said to a dying man? I feel sorry for him.

She watched as he struggled to reached the side of his bed.

"Answer me or I'll press the button. I made it clear that Abby was the only one I trusted. Where's your badge? If you're trying to sell something, get out! Nobody wants what you have."

Did he just call me a hooker?

Sara hands shot to her hips.

"Excuse me," she challenged. "What are you suggesting?"

Garrison vigorously pressed the call button and

shouted, "Abby! Abby, I think a dealer or runner is in my room!"

Dammit, Sara! Stop thinking he's the same man. He's trying to stay sober.

The alarm began bleeping faster.

"I'm not a dealer," she shouted.

"You're not Abby!"

Abigale rushed in and pressed a large red button on his cardiac monitor.

"I'm right here," she said while pulling his hand away from the call button.

"Do you know this woman?"

"Yes."

"Oh . . . sorry. I uh, I thought you were trying to sneak something in and—I'm sorry if I was rude." He looked up at Abigale and back to Sara. His pale face brightened as he said, "My name is Garrison James, I'm an alcoholic. It has been—"

"No worries," interrupted Sara. She could tell he was embarrassed. "It's completely understandable. You didn't expect to wakeup to anyone but Abigale." She shrugged her shoulders and added, "I get it, and I'm sorry if I startled you."

Garrison's eyes widened.

"You look a lot like..." He tilted his head to the side and asked, "Do I know you? Are you related to Lila James?"

"That's my cue," chimed Abigale.

Sara's mind shouted, *Oh my God she's going to leave!*

"Your cue?" questioned Garrison. "Your cue for what?"

"To give you some privacy." She patted Garrison's hand. "I won't be far."

"Why are you doing that?"

Abigale ignored Garrison's question and turned to Sara. She said, "You've got this. We both know you're ready."

"I don't know how to begin," admitted Sara.

"That's easy," replied Abigale. She winked at Sara before turning to Garrison. "I'd like you to meet Ms. Sara James." She lightly patted Garrison's foot and said with a light chuckle, "And this old grump here is Garrison James."

Without skipping a beat, she turned and left.

"Sara? Sara, is ... is it really you?"

It took her a moment, before she nervously replied, "Yes."

"Thank you so much for coming to..." He paused for a moment. Sara was about to respond, but before she could, he asked, "Did you come to see me, or were you forced? I mean . . . I'm glad you came, but nobody has the right to force you."

"I came on my own." She looked away and admitted, "I had to."

"Why?"

Like Abigale said, the best respect to give is honesty. Be honest, we both deserve it.

She slowly walked towards him and said, "I need answers."

Chapter Thirty

Chapter Thirty-One

Sara watched in silence while Garrison's hand fumbled with the buttons on the side of his bed.

What is he doing? Does he want Abigale to come back?

"Where is it?" Garrison mumbled.

"Where is what? Just what are you trying to do," she blurted in a low whisper, "Abigale left so we could talk!"

Weak and exhausted, his hand dropped to his side.

"I was trying to sit up."

Dammit, her mind shouted as she rushed over to assist.

She pressed the up button on the side of her bed and muttered, "Let me know when to stop."

The bed slowly rose. Once he was on a safe angle, he said, "That's good."

Sara's mind raced as she continued to stand by his side.

How do I start? He doesn't look anything like what I pictured. I'm supposed to be honest but I don't know . . . I don't know anything.

Nurse Brooks eyed the second hand on her watch. Time passed without either saying a word. After three full minutes, she marched to the threshold of his room and gave three light taps.

"Abby," said Garrison. "You don't have to knock."

"I know, but you just woke and I have a job to do," she said as she walked to the tray that held a small jug of ice water. She filled a foam cup, applied a lid and straw, and then handed it to Sara. "He needs to drink. Would you mind?"

"Not at all," replied Sara.

"I don't have Alzheimer," Garrison said with a light chuckle.

"You could have fooled me," Abigale teased.

Sara laughed as she twisted the straw forward and brought the cup to his mouth.

Feeling relieved, Garrison's eyes danced between the two. He was grateful for Abigale, and elated to see his daughter.

Abigale crossed her arms and lightly tapped her foot.

"Come on you ol' grump."

Garrison chuckled. He loved when she teased him. It made him feel alive and loved.

"Okay, okay, I'll drink."

The hearty nurse lightly brushed her hand across Sara's shoulder and whispered, "You see what I mean, he's no longer under the influence. You are fortunate because this is your opportunity to see the man your mother loved."

"Thanks, Abby," she whispered.

Abigale nodded.

Chapter Thirty-One

"If you need me, I'll be in the hall."

Garrison took a long slow drink. He purposely took his time to gain his confidence. When he finished, he pressed his head back on his pillow and let out a heavy sigh.

"Would you like some more?" asked Sara.

"No. I'm fine. Please, Sara, have a seat."

She noticed how dark his room seemed.

"I'll open the curtains first."

"Please don't, the lights cause strain to my weakened eyes," he said. "As you know, the doctors have already I don't have much time and cannot waste another moment."

"Alright."

"First—I need to tell you how very sorry I am for making our lives harder than they needed to be."

Harder? Now that's an understatement.

"The reason I tried to contact you is because I didn't want to fail you again."

"Again?" She questioned, "What do you mean by 'again'?"

She instantly looked away when she heard the revulsion in her tone.

"I know as a father I wasn't there for you, but that doesn't mean I didn't love you." He let out a weak huff. "The reason I called you was to inform you I have cancer, and since your mother died of cancer, I wanted to warn you."

"Warn me—warn me of what?"

"The cancer," he stressed. "You have twice the danger."

He struggled to take in a deeper breath. "Please, be vigilant. Tell your physician about your mother and me, and see them regularly." He released the remaining air and smiled as he took in a jagged breath. After a second heavy release, he inhaled another rough breath and said, "I know I'm weak and pathetic, but this is what I've dreamt of—the day I could see my little girl again."

"I don't know if I could do this," Sara whispered.

"To do what?"

"Be your little girl." Sara stood and began pacing. "I came here for answers." She turned and glared into his eyes. "I need to know why? Why did you start drinking, why did you—just why!"

"I was weak! An invisible demon named cancer was taking my wife and I couldn't see it to fight it." His breathing continued to struggle while he explained, "It took every penny we had to make Lila comfortable, and I was scared. I was losing the construction company, and I didn't know how to tell her." He looked away from Sara and to the only picture he brought and back. "How could I tell the one person who was willing to give me everything that I failed? That we might not be able to pay for her next prescription, or that our daughter wouldn't be able to go to the dentist—that we couldn't buy a full week of groceries if she chose to give chemo another try."

She thought it over.

No, I cannot feel for him until I get answers. I know it would be hard, but he continued drinking after she died. How could he do that when I was still there, his only child and family?

"For thirteen weeks I failed. I drowned that failure in wine and beer. When I lost my wife I didn't know where to turn and—"

"No!" Sara interrupted. "You continued drinking after she died. How could you?" She noticed No matter how hard she tried to control her emotions her body deceived her. She wiped her tears away and shouted, "You left me alone! The day mom died, I needed you and you weren't there! It was as if you died too! I really needed my father! For years . . . I had to take care and clean up after your mess!"

"It was my only source of comfort. When I drank, I forgot."

"You forgot! The day my mother died, I lost both parents. I was an instant orphan taking care of a drunk."

"Sara, Sara!" He started coughing hysterically. "I—I was," his words were choppy. After fighting in a full breath, he cried out, "You are absolutely right! I didn't know how to handle your mother's death!" He continued gasping for air. "She was my world. Together we created a smaller and nearly identical version of her. Lila and I were so proud and it was hard—hard to look at you and not miss your mother."

Sara realized he was crying and tried to find a box of Kleenex.

"I wish I could give you answers but I can't. All I can

do is tell you the truth, and that is how deeply sorry and thankful I am."

She froze steps away from the Kleenex box.

"You're thankful?"

"Yes. I'm thankful for your strength, and for Valerie and Kyle rescuing you from what I had become. I was a cowardly monster that tormented and abused my beloved daughter. I'm not asking for forgiveness. I want you to know that I thank you. You had the strength to leave. It forced me to face what I'd become and fight it. I am no longer that man, I haven't been for over a decade, and if it wasn't for you..." He fell silent.

She spun around and saw him struggle to wipe his tears.

Kleenexes, we both need them!

It was the first time she had no doubt her father recognized what he had done. While retrieving the box and returning to his side. She finally felt at peace with her past.

"I believe you," she whispered while holding a tissue out to him.

Garrison reached past the tissue and grasped her hand. He gave a genuine smile and said, "You are a blessing. I lost sight of that, but not since the day or sobered and every since. I know who and what you are, and, Sara, your mother and I couldn't be more proud."

Sara gripped his hand in returned and smiled. She felt as if a huge burden had been lifted and she could finally breathe.

Chapter Thirty-One

"Thank you, Father."

"There is no need to thank me, you saved me. You, my darling angel, saved me." The confrontation had weakened him. After a short moment to catch his breath, he admitted, "I need rest, but I'm afraid to sleep because my dream has finally come true."

Frozen by his side, Sara stood holding his hand and waited until he was in a restful sleep. When the machines and his breathing regulated, she released his hand and shot across the room to retrieve the chair. The moment she returned to his side, she sat down, took his hand and watched him sleep.

The room was silent. To Sara, everything felt right.

"I'm sorry, Mitch," said Abigale. "It's been nearly an hour since they talked. I'm not sure if she is awake."

An hour really? Why is Mitch here and how did Abigale know his name? What am I thinking? He told me he was on the visitor's list.

"Is it alright for another guest?" asked Abigale. "Garrison made sure Mitch was added to the list. He is a good friend. Garrison thinks of him as a son."

"Yes. I know him," Sara whispered with a nod.

Mitch walked in and smiled at Sara.

"Hey," he whispered. "How are you guys?"

"We're good."

He looked around the room. When he did not see what he was looking for, he left.

That was odd, thought Sara.

When he stopped at the door and leaned out. Sara held her breath so she could hear what Mitch had to say.

"It's Abby right?"

"Yes."

"Pops cherished a picture. I don't see it on his bedside table. Pops keeps that picture with him at all times, he couldn't go a day without it. Do you know where his personal items are?"

"I know what you're talking about. He had it in the bed with him. It might be under his blanket." A short pause of silence followed, Sara leaned forward at the same moment she heard Abigale whisper, "I'll help you look for it."

"No need," replied Mitch. "The room is small and I don't want Sara to feel claustrophobic. If I can't find it—" He shrugged. "I'll leave the room so that you and Sara can take a gander."

Lost for words, Sara sat still and watched as Mitch searched the bed. When he pulled the covers back, there laid the picture, facedown on Garrisons chest.

"Here it is," whispered Mitch. He slowly turned it towards Sara. "It's Pops' security blanket. He says he wouldn't have survived without it. Do you recognize this?"

Sara recalled the photograph.

Wow . . . that has to be one of the last picnic days we spent as a family. Mom was so sick but she insisted we do it.

"Yes. I remember the day. In my memory, Mom was

healthy. I see now that she was beautiful and weak," she admitted.

"Pops said she was stubborn and refuse to miss your traditional family picnic." Mitch turned the picture around and smiled.

"Mom was the glue that held us together."

"I wish I got to meet her. You look like her." He admitted in a low whisper, "You're both breathtakingly beautiful."

She blushed as she looked down at her hands.

Chapter Thirty-Two

The final two weeks of Garrison's life was short. Each second meant the world to him and Sara.

Garrison was thankful to see and get to know his daughter.

Sara was grateful for the opportunity to get to know her him. She often wondered what her mother saw, if he was different from the man she remember.

He was.

On evenings when the pain was too much for Garrison, he insisted she go to Mitch's house and not a hotel. He knew the two had built a friendship, and trusted they would continue to help each other long after he had passed.

Sara and Mitch did not mind. They spent those nights talking. It was the foundation to a friendship much stronger than Garrison could have hoped for.

A light tap woke Sara. She opened her eyes and saw Mitch standing over her with a phone in hand.

"What time is it?" she asked.

Chapter Thirty-Two

She was sleeping in his guestroom. The one room in his home he hardly used. He frantically looked around the room. "I don't know," he admitted.

"You seem shaken, is every thing alright?"

"Abby's on the phone. She sounds concerned."

They rushed to his side. That afternoon, Garrison passed away.

Chapter Thirty-Three

The day of Garrison's funeral arrived.

Father Daniels agreed to conduct the sermon and prayers. During the final viewing, he politely pulled Sara into a private room.

"During the ceremony, I would like to invite you up to share a few words."

What do I say? Before the viewings, I didn't know half those people. Sure, I knew Aunt Valerie and Uncle Kyle were coming, but I hardly know the rest. Most are from his A.A. meetings.

Father Daniels placed his hand on her shoulder.

"This is a difficult time, and I don't mean to rush you, but I need to know before we begin."

She politely declined.

After the viewing, Father Daniels opened the curtain and escorted her to the front pew.

Sara remained calm. Even after he mentioned her mother, and how he did not think he would have to repeat the same service for her father so soon after her mother's death.

Chapter Thirty-Three

Instead of hanging on his words, she focused on the reasons she appreciated Father Daniels.

He's practically family. Father Daniels is the one who married my parents. He ran and still runs our church, and if he didn't read my father's seven sacraments, I wouldn't have known he had everything, including his funeral, in order before he entered Spring Time Meadows. We're really lucky to have Father Daniels. Even when our family fell apart, he could see the good in each of us, and he had faith in us. He knew we would find our way.

Sara was surprised when she looked up and saw Father Daniels' hand outstretched before her. In a robotic fashion, she stood and followed his lead.

When they arrived at the gravesite, she stayed by the car and watched as a small group of friends and family gathered outside the casket.

Out of nowhere, Sara felt a burst of confidence.

It's the right thing to do, she thought as marched past the crowd. She stopped at the front of Garrison's casket and faced everyone. *I owe this to us.*

"Thank you for coming." Her tone shook as her emotions tried to take control. She fought it. "For years I referred to Garrison James as 'the monster'."

Gasps in the crowd caught her attention.

I will not succumb to their shock! She reminded herself. *I will speak the truth and not sugarcoat it.*

Needing a moment regain control, Sara looked down at her trembling hands and took in a calming breath.

Chapter Thirty-Three

I have to stay focused and remember how the truth set us free. The least I can do is share our story. It could help free another family.

She looked up from her hands and slowly scanned the crowd. She stopped the moment Mitch's eyes met hers.

Mitch was her rock.

He made it!

That morning, one of his neighbors called. They begged him to help. Their mare went into labor the night before. Mitch tried to back out of it and recommend another vet, but they refused. They trusted Mitch, and admitted they feared losing both.

He is a walking book. I can tell the mare and foal made it.

Mitch weaved through the small crowd and joined her side.

"Thanks for making it," she whispered.

"It was a close call," he admitted while placing his hand on her shoulder. "Please continue."

She slowly nodded.

"Alcohol owned us. As fast as my father consumed it, it consumed us. Like a demon, it sucked the life out of us. It left us with pain, fear, and misery. For years, I was lost in a pit of what I thought was eternal damnation. On the inside, you could say I was broken, and I was. Until two extraordinary people stepped in and gave me a home. They loved, cared, and did what they could to protect me." Her eyes danced between Kyle and Valerie. "They did everything in their power to shield me from my father. They didn't know he stopped drinking and the monster was no longer around. I don't hold them responsible, I understand and thank them."

Realizing she mentioned the monster, she looked away from her aunt and uncle and addressed the crowd.

"When Garrison James drank, he became a monster. Nobody knew that monster, except me, and when I asked for help . . . nobody listened." She shrugged and said, "Maybe I was too young for them to take seriously. Those I spoke with told me to give him time. To be patient." She paused when she heard her own words.

"I'm sorry, my child," said Father Daniels.

"Don't be," she insisted. "I'm here to share our story. To help bring awareness. To say goodbye to my father and . . . and to thank every single one of you."

Mitch rubbed her shoulder.

"I'd like to express my thanks to Aunt Valerie and Uncle Kyle for providing me with the opportunity to live again." Her eyes watered as they bounced between each visitor. "And I'd like to thank you. When my father stopped drinking, you supported him. You helped him become the man he once—" She caught herself. "That was wrong. You helped him find and return to the man my mother fell in love with. The REAL Garrison James, and thanks to your support, he never gave up. I was blessed with the opportunity to see and get to know him, my dad." She struggled to wipe her tears away.

Mitch cleared his throat.

Chapter Thirty-Three

Everyone, including Sara turned to him.

"Pops and I spent a lot of time together. When he learned the cancer had won, he asked me to promise I would not morn his death, but celebrate his life. It was an easy promise." Mitch slid his hand off Sara's shoulder and cupped her hand. "We invite you to join us in the celebration. Food and drinks are available at the James' house. The doors are open to anyone who wishes to share stories about the good times they share with Pops."

Nurse Abigale Brooks was the first to move. She stepped up and placed a rose on the casket.

"I already have the address," she said. "I'm looking forward to sharing."

After everyone left, Mitch placed his rose on the casket and whispered, "Shall I wait by the car or would you prefer the house?"

"It's alright," she replied as she released her rose. She slid her fingertips across the foot of the casket and whispered, "Goodbye, Daddy. Don't forget to give Mom a hug, and tell her I love her."

Dedication

To my wonderful husband Jeremy and our three beautiful children Paul, Michael, and Consuelo. They provided continued support and understanding while I worked hard towards publishing this story. I love you all.

To my family and friends, as well as expressing my deepest thanks to God for his many blessings.

I want to extend best wishes to my beta readers. Thank you for your suggestions, you helped make Closure shine.

Writer's 750-Group and all the talented writers within. Thank you for the continued inspiration and for helping me take that first step.

A big shout out to my SNHU (writing group). Thank you for supporting and encouraging me to work on my craft. You provided insightful writing prompts and tremendous feedback.

To the many authors and writers who have encouraged me throughout the years. You know who you are, and so do I—I would not have taken this broad step without you.

Dedication

Last, but not least, to all of my readers. You are the reason I continue writing.

Thank you,

Sylvia Stein

Acknowledgments

ACKNOWLEDGEMENTS

My editor: Due to her heavy workload, she prefers to remain anonymous. I thank you for the countless words of encouragement, blunt feedback, and for pushing me to work hard.

Cover design provided by Natasha Brown

Disclaimer

Disclaimer

Author Bio

ABOUT THE AUTHOR

Author Sylvia Stein began her path to writing when she joined the Writer's 750-Group on Linked.

She continued her journey by creating short stories. Sixteen of which were published in the Giant Tales Anthology series.

While obtaining her Masters degree at Southern New Hampshire University, Stein continued building a solid foundation with her colleagues. They encouraged her to continue writing.

It was there that the premise for Closure was born.

With the help of her editor, Closure grew from an idea to a full novella.

Stein said, "Closure is my first solo project. I am excited to share this and many more."

Author pic